DEAR LOVE

A Memoir | Collective Poetry | Inspirational Literature

Front Cover Photo and Cover Design
By
Jai QuietStorm

DEAR LOVE

A Memoir | Collective Poetry | Inspirational Literature

Jai QuietStorm

Published in the United States

By

'N Gratitude Publishing Company

www.NGratitude.net

ISBN 978-0-9833150-3-2

Printed in the United States of America

Hard Cover - First Edition

DEDICATION

To my Heavenly Creator; to my mother,

who from day one has loved me as only a mother can

— unconditionally.

To all my loved ones and anyone who's ever fought for love,

lost the battle and yet still never gave up the war…

Like many faithful writers, artists and performers,

I am fearlessly, faithfully, and patiently awaiting that big break,

that life-defining piece and most of all my happy ending…

~ *JQS*

CONTENTS

You may not be her first, her last, or her only. She loved before she may love again. But if she loves you now, what else matters? She's not perfect - you aren't either, and the two of you may never be perfect together but if she can make you laugh, cause you to think twice, and admit to being human and making mistakes, hold onto her and give her the most you can. She may not be thinking about you every second of the day, but she will give you a part of her that she knows you can break - her heart. So don't hurt her, don't change her, don't analyze and don't expect more than she can give. Smile when she makes you happy, let her know when she makes you mad, and miss her when she's not there.

Ever so often in your life, I truly believe, you find someone who can completely turn your world around. You tell them things that you've never shared with another soul and they absorb everything you say and actually want to hear more. You share hopes for the future, dreams that will never come true, goals that were never achieved and the many disappointments life has thrown at you. When something wonderful happens, you can't wait to tell them about it, knowing they will share in your excitement. They are not embarrassed to cry with you when you are hurting or laugh with you when you make a fool of yourself. Never do they hurt your feelings or make you feel like you are not good enough, but rather they build you up and show you the things about yourself that make you special and even beautiful. There is never any pressure, jealousy or competition but only a quiet calmness when they are around. You can be yourself and not worry about what they will think of you because they love you for who you are.

The things that seem insignificant to most people such as a note, song or walk become invaluable treasures kept safe in your heart to cherish forever. Memories of your childhood come back and are so clear and vivid it's like being young again. Colours seem brighter and more brilliant. Laughter seems part of daily life where before it was infrequent or didn't exist at all. A phone call or two during the day helps to get you through a long day's work and always brings a smile to your face. In their presence, there's no need for continuous conversation, but you find you're quite content in just having them nearby. Things that never interested you before become fascinating because you know they are important to this person who is so special to you. You think of this person on every occasion and in everything you do. Simple things bring them to mind like a pale blue sky, gentle wind or even a storm cloud on the horizon.

You open your heart knowing that there's a chance it may be broken one day and in opening your heart, you experience a love and joy that you never dreamed possible. You find that being vulnerable is the only way to allow your heart to feel true pleasure that's so real it scares you. You find strength in knowing you have a true friend and possibly a soul mate who will remain loyal to the end. Life seems completely different, exciting and worthwhile. Your hope and security is in knowing that they are a part of your life.

~ Bob Marley ...(R.I.P)

LOVE LETTER TO MY READERS

(Preface)

Dear Lovers,

Isn't it ironic how the matchmakers can't seem to find true love, the psychologists tend to have more private issues than their patients, and how our religious figures appear to hold the darkest secrets and most corrupt pasts. It trails back on that "good guys always finish last" aphorism that has shown to hold some truth in our society. For these individuals are professionally trained and skilled experts in their practices and still fall short in their intimate lives. Does that leave little hope for the rest of us amateurs who pursue personal success? Or does it just bare the fact that in the midst of what we know, what we do and how good we are at what we do, the reality is—despite age, experience, education or status—we all have "something greater" to learn about life and the people of this world; and in order to accept and understand these wisdoms we have to first be willing to fail in order to succeed in our careers, beliefs and especially in love.

Relationships are like plants—you have to water and provide sunlight for them to blossom, flourish and to essentially grow. Whether families, friendships, romantic affairs or lustful rendezvous—every relationship, if desired to succeed, has to be nourished, invested and guided in order to reach its full potential. Now I'm no specialized guru in the study of love, nor do I possess an esteemed doctorate in relational psychology or human studies. Nonetheless, if there's one thing I've acquired in my 23 years of existence, it's a heavy share of broken hearts [and with more to come]; and I bet if you ask anyone who firsthand experienced love and pain in its rarest forms, they would tell you that the wisdom and insight you gain from those inevitable, intrinsic processes are more powerful and valuable than any level of degree, or tangible honor of expertise could ever be. And though I'm not a scholar on love—who is? For it's become my understanding that in understanding love, this wisdom isn't acquired solely based upon your knowledge, background or time but your individual experience; for everyone has a story to tell—this is just mine.

I could spit this philosophical, reflective rhetoric all day but that's not my aim in this prelusive love letter. I rather aspire to convey to you a piece of who I am, why I write and what purpose this all serves. With that being said, allow me to formally introduce myself as Jai "QuietStorm" Stephens—culturally enriched Southern, modern-Renaissance-80s-baby; faithful connoisseur of romance, passion and love; sensual solicitor of ineffable auras, captivating vibes and artful affinities; and a future avant-garde intellect, writer, artist and speaker of our time. Au contraire, I am perfectly imperfect in every sense and form, or else I wouldn't have the impassioned material to write these words I speak to you now. However, I am an absolute product of the beauty that resurfaces from the ashes and am thereby a rising survivor of life's love, pain, pleasures, blood, sweat and tears. I truly believe that the only way to conquer, cultivate and prosper in life and love is through the nature of the relationships we pursue and secure. But first, we must confront and defy our demons of fear, insecurity and misery (which we all possess), because it's these subconscious barriers that often force us to become self-inflictive, and restrains us from moving forward and escaping our darkness. For with the exception of God, we are our only saviors and light shines brightest in the dark.

Lovers, the bittersweet reality is simply this—we thrive on love! We are at our best when we are intimate, appreciated, impassioned, needed, encouraged, recognized, acknowledged, praised and catered to—and despite ethnicity, gender, spirituality, sexuality or political agenda—we, as human beings, all feed off the power to give and to receive love; and in the same, so easily decline without it. For the universe's wealthiest, wisest, strongest, fastest, most attractive women and men have NOTHING without someone to share those attributes with. It's an inevitable truth, in which many of us fail to understand or accept, but it is what it is. I was brought up to believe that God is all, and in everything He is especially LOVE. In that understanding, I grew to love Love as genuinely and wholeheartedly as a child could. I sought and practiced its ways in everything and everyone I pursued. Each time I was exposed to the touch, taste, sight, smell and sound of its grace, like an ill-nourished soul I yearned for more. While others perceived and deemed my vulnerability and faithfulness to these emotions as weakness and naïveté, I wore that innate altruism and passion as a spiritual badge and continued to indulge in those heartfelt desires.

Unfortunately, in the imperfect world that we live in, with that much openness and vulnerability it was only a matter of time before those heartfelt aspirations were taken advantage of—only to be overturned by distress, affliction and resentment. Lovers, ***shaking my head, exhaling…*** that "love jones" is a powerful, merciless and supernatural force. One so vehemently unrelenting that when it finally grabs a hold of your soul and comes down on your conscious, it's nothing short of a quiet storm—an enamored outbreak and blinding whirlwind so vigorously incontrollable that the flooding downpour, if not cautious, can cause some to drown in their own passion. So why do we love—why take the risk of drowning, being broken, lost and confused? Is it to have a sense of belonging—of comfort, or to simply have someone to call our own? Maybe we feel this pre-natal longing to feel significant, to feel desired, to feel like we matter. Like when we leave this earth we won't be forgotten—but remembered for not what we accomplished, not where we came from but sincerely for how we made others feel….

So in this conveyance of love letters, prose, poetry and song, I present my "firsts" [first crush, first intimacy, first love, first burn, first mistake and first epiphany] in hopes that I inspire, stimulate and satisfy your nourishment of LOVE. In my prime I've been blessed with the opportunity to both love and be loved. To fall in and out; to win and lose; to fight and get my ass kicked so hard and so low that I questioned my worth, and more detrimentally—God's existence. For they say the best achievement in life is to love yourself, love God and love others.

So yes, I've had the privilege of experiencing the greatest gift known to exist; and throughout my relational escapades I've absorbed and internalized some essential skills, lessons and values. Along my journey I've documented my inner most thoughts, feelings, fears, joys, pains, passions and pleasures from the depths of my soul. I've even managed to salvage some responsive pieces of long-lost lovers professing impassioned reciprocations.

Furthermore, it is my sincere belief that in every relationship we "endure" there is an undeniable soundtrack of musical identity that embodies all the emotions, trials, and ups and downs of your time with that individual. In that, each of my experiences featured in this memoir follows a track list of songs that vividly and painstakingly remind me solely of my affinity at that particular time in my life. Each chapter engages a love letter expressing and divulging a unique situation with a unique person under even more unique circumstances. The poetry tells stories and the stories read as poetry.

In so many words—as many of you can relate—my love life thus far has been quite unorthodox and unapologetic. So lovers, readers and even non-believers, I present to you this collective piece of intimate love letters not only to entice, entertain or comfort your ideals on love, but to re-open your senses to a reformed depiction of love, passion and pain, in pursuit of your gain and seeking of a greater appreciation and devotion in your present and future relationships and beliefs. So in my hopes of cathecting your minds, hearts and spirits I give to you a piece of my own—my peace, faith, character, desires, guilt, heartache, bliss and essentially my love are all here for your rapprochement.

My wish is that my story, my journey and my truth will instill a refreshment of courage, will and purpose to love again, to love better or to even love for the first time. Coming from a historical mentally, physically and emotionally enslaved culture that would rather sit self-indulgent and idle and watch our people fail, than to support and uplift our spirits; from a generational society that would rather disown their children, their own flesh and blood than to forgive and agree to disagree with their lifestyles;

and raised in an era where money, power, respect, sex, drugs and status are all we eat, sleep and s— (defecate); I write this as a preliminary step in becoming the change I hope to see in our world.

So I pray that these stories, these experiences and most definitely this poetry evokes a stronger sense of self, of the world and essentially the people whom you care about most. So take a deep breath, relax and close your eyes because, ***DEAR LOVE***, life is too short to miss your chance for a great happy ending.

Love will never come to an end. Prophecies will cease;

tongues of ecstasy will fall silent; knowledge will vanish.

For our knowledge and our prophecy alike are partial,

and the partial vanishes when wholeness comes.

When I was a child I spoke like a child, thought like a child,

reasoned like a child;

but when I grew up I finished with childish things.

At present we see only puzzling reflections in a mirror,

but one day we shall see face to face.

My knowledge now is partial; then it will be whole,

like God's knowledge of me.

There are three things that last forever; faith, hope, and love;

and the greatest of the three is love.

~ 1 Corinthians 13

Bonus Chapter

"GENESIS OF LOVE" *(Ma)*

Soundtracks "Mama" - Boyz II Men |
"Lean On Me" - Kirk Franklin |
"Fly Like a Bird" - Mariah Carey |

Quote *"All that I am or ever hope to be, I owe to my angel, my mother."*

~ Abraham Lincoln

I believe that every person on this earth at some point in their childhood—no matter how good or bad, high or low or rich or poor, just wanted to make their mother proud of them. They say that the way your lover loves respects and honors their mother is the way that they will always treat you. For a mother's love is ingrained in us; in who we once were, where we go and who we will grow to become for forever.

As our mothers are our actual first sight of love; our first sound, smell, touch and taste of love, all our senses, our desires and beliefs initially stem and are inspired through these women who brought us into the world. And though they are as imperfect as all God's creatures, they are divinely purposeful in so many aspects aside from giving us life. These women teach us even before we or they are aware that we're being taught or taught to. Human contact, affection, comfort and attachment are our first associations with love as infants, and scientific studies show that without it early on and throughout life development, we won't thrive and sometimes even die.

The powerful connection between a mother and child is so strong that whenever a child is hurt or scared or lost, their initial reaction is to call or reach out to her. As we all are unique, we all don't have the privilege of growing up with those motherly experiences, as some of us either never knew our mothers or our memory of them isn't the most memorable. Nevertheless, we all have that innate desire to love and be loved and it all started with the first life, the first being and the first woman you ever came in contact with—your mother.

July 24, 2012

Dear Ma,

I find myself randomly angry. Not intentionally, but it's evident that my unhappiness has got the best of me and I'm trapped in a space where I can't even control it. My attitude is ruining my relationship with the one person I can't live without—my mama. It seems you think I hate you, am ashamed to be yours and that's far from the truth; and yet I act as so—like I'm better than you. When really all it boils down to is my insecurity and resentment for still being under your roof. I can't remember the last time I witnessed you cry. I'm sure you cry to yourself because of me. I'm sure I piss you off sometimes and I feel as though you think I'm wasting my time, my gifts and my life—drowning in my potential.

Deep down I know you ONLY want what is best for me and my future—what responsible parent doesn't; but more importantly, you want to see your child happy and I haven't been that—at least not in your eyes. Because all I do is continue to distance myself from you and our family, isolating myself in your household, as if I'm a prisoner. You constantly remind me in your frustration that I'm free to leave at anytime; but WE both know there is no one out there who will ever care, love and provide for me the way that only a mother can.

The truth is that I'm most disappointed in my failures at my vulnerability, and where it has placed me. You'd think I would know better by now to listen to my mother rather than idle advice from associates, lovers and inexperienced comrades. But they say I'm still young and have a WHOLE lot more to learn but that's neither an excuse nor adequate enough reason to be ignorant or irresponsible, not with the way you raised me.

Physically I still feel like the 18 year-young high school graduate I was five years ago. But emotionally, I sense the aging far more. I always say if LOVE was a professional career I'd be at the top of my game, with a competitive seven-figure salary, full benefits—hell, even federal government clearance ***laughing**;** a billionaire before my 30th birthday and perhaps even a Pulitzer Prize winner in the field. But in the real world, love is something that though it can be taught, is rather hard to learn as far as skill level or expertise. With love comes wisdom, and the only way to acquire wisdom is through openness and experience.

At times, Ma, I honestly feel like love's fool. It seems that I give so much and receive so little in return. Not that you should always expect to be reciprocated but the effort is priceless. Yet in reality I truly have NOTHING to complain about. I'm blessed beyond measure: I'm sheltered, clothed, fed, quenched, physically and mentally healthy, and able to do whatever I desire. I guess what I seek is a second chance and another opportunity to love and be loved—the right way.

If I could obtain that I promise Ma, I would leave all these materialistic, tangible distractions behind, to serve God first and foremost. I feel as though I need an escape, even if that means being alone for the rest of my life. I mean it has to be better and feel less like a waste of time than pursuing these individuals who don't want real love. I just need to go, to run and to flee to a purposed life. Maybe a change of scenery, an independent life away from everything I once knew and loved…then maybe then will I be able to find my joy again.

When I stopped seeing my mother with the eyes of a child, I saw the woman who helped me give birth to myself.

~ Nancy Friday

Love, your only daughter,
~ Jai Nichol

P.S. Ma,

For as long as I can remember you have always been there for me; from my first little league game, to every formal school dance and art show; to graduation—from Kindergarten to college; from my first broken bone to my first major surgery, sunrise to sundown you were there, never ever missing a single beat.

As a single mother and family of just us two, you influenced me in ways I wouldn't learn in a full functioning family. I learned early on the values of independence, patience, virtue, self-respect, faith and self-less-ness. You distinguished the rights from wrongs, instilled the significance of a cultivating relationship versus religion with God, and essentially how to protect, provide and value my gifts, knowledge and self. You revealed a world of supreme possibilities and assured me that if I worked hard, honored God and stayed faithful that one day I'd be blessed with the opportunity to pursue my wildest dreams. You uplifted me, inspired a desire and passion to travel and explore the world beyond my own culture, beliefs and understanding. You wanted more for me which taught me to need more for myself. You taught me how and when to serve and submit and then led me to be a leader versus a follower… I owe my humility, modesty and patience to you and for that I thank you for it made me who I am today.

I grew up watching you maintain a positive attitude in the midst of struggle, managing a strong work ethic while facing challenges and continually putting others before yourself. I came to accept that inheritance of self-sacrifice as a blessing and a curse, but after gaining some wisdom realized that life is much greater than just me and that we were put on this earth to serve those who need us. Through your strong will, spiritual foundation and assertive perseverance you showed me that I define my life in the ways that I choose to respond to defeat… you never let me fail even when I failed.

Speaking on inheritance, you also passed on an early appreciation of soul music, particularly that of the spiritually gifted and artistically talented R&B crooner, Maxwell. In that I grasped and assimilated the natural essence of emotively poetic rhythms, lyrics and sounds and how if combined perfectly with a timeless, sensual voice it could evoke and speak volumes of healing, peace, passion and wisdom. You planted that artistic seed in me from the time I could sing and motion along and that creativity will forever be imprinted in me from your musical influence. One of the most valuable things you taught me about love, life and myself is that God makes no mistakes and though it may seem unfair, illogical or just insensible...that good or bad, everything and everyone throughout your life has a season and serves a greater purpose. With age and experience this truth becomes so much more valid and its one of those things that in hard times, helps maintain the sanity and keep the peace...through every job, every class, every heartbreak, every crash and every life-changing experience THAT was one of your greatest lessons of all because you showed me how to heal, adapt, improvise and be stronger than yesterday.

Even though we're not as close as I'd like us to be the older I get the more internally and externally I am reminded that I am my mother's child and that makes me happy because believe it or not I am always proud of you. Sometimes even as adult children we don't praise or thank or simply honor our loved ones as much as we should especially our mothers. We tend to take for granted the fact that they nurtured, supported and guided our lives for so long that a surreal part of us believes that they'll always be there...until their gone; oh we can't even fathom that. Not the one person who has always been constant and real in my life. There's no chance that she would ever abandon, desert or neglect me. No chance that she would disown me. Not now; not ever…it just isn't a reality until that one unfortunate day that it is.

Some time ago an older woman once looked me earnestly in my eyes and said if your mother is still alive you take care of her. You love her and honor her with every bone in your body and hair on your head. Respect her wishes and make her happy for as long as God allows because you only get ONE and there is no one on this earth who will ever be capable of loving and taking care of you like that woman. As if her words struck immediate lucidity in my veins, I loved my mother a little harder from then on because lovers come, lovers go and though God is always only a prayer away there is nothing like a mother's love.

Mama exhorted her children at every opportunity

to jump at de sun. We might not land on de sun,

but at least we would get off the ground.

~ Zora Neale Hurston

I.

"TEENAGE LOVE AFFAIR" *(Desire)*

Soundtracks "Diamonds & Pearls" - Prince |
"Believe" - Raheem Devaughn |
"Fortunate" - Maxwell |

Quote *"Thy most important lesson in life is to learn how to give out love, and to let it come in."*

~ Morrie Schwartz

Dear Desire,

(Summer)

Overwhelmed in nostalgic moments, I've always embraced the thought of myself as a magnanimous lover and yet in my past relationships I've tended to come up short as nothing more than a compeer to those whom I sincerely wanted more with.

Fresh out of high school, approaching my 18th birthday, en route to one of the top internationally, academic and athletic, universities on a full scholarship, little did I know that you would be undeniably the first of all relational firsts. Uncompromised; unexpected; unpredicted; that summer upon my induction in what is rightfully considered to be the best four years of your life, opened my eyes and exposed my heart to emotions that only existed in novels, poetry, films and my imagination. Like many first moments, you captured my innocence in an undeniable fashion that can never be imitated or duplicated. What made the experience even more unprecedented and pure was the simple fact that I've always believed that I was a "first" for you as well. Maybe not a first attraction or crush as mine but I most confidently served as a first connection and interaction in which you once confessed I was "the first person you ever feared giving your heart to." Ah, to be young and infatuated ***sighs***…it's a newly terrifying and yet electrifying feeling that can be wholeheartedly experienced only once in a lifetime.

I must admit, as inexperienced and unsophisticated as our teenage love affair presented itself to be, it progressed profoundly and at the passionately, incontrollable rate that most youthful affinities grow. *Desire*, you unknowingly taught me one of my first lessons of love, affection and vulnerability; and even though you pushed, pulled and fought away from every burning inclination inside of you to admit that you had concrete, romantic feelings for me, I still couldn't resist the addictively, foreign cupidity to be with you. I was sprung.

That first crush is like that first inebriation, that first taste of your favorite food or that first arousal…it's a consuming, emotional high you can't explain, you can't escape, and if you allow it, it'll take you on a mental adventure so wild your daydreams will become reality. And yet as with all things, especially good things, they come to an end. *Desire*, you were no exception, and as my first premature lesson, you taught me the value of letting go of what never "was" to begin with.

June 4, 2007

Love Fiend (Part I)

I'll start by saying that I trust what we have will be something eternal so that we can live until our spirits leave this earth and even then I truly believe our souls will find each other yet again so that we may continue this infinite love/

I wish to go highs and lows with you that no one else has ever gone with you before/

I want to kiss away your tears, drive away your fears, comfort your mind, and stimulate your soul/

I want to whisper soft, sweet nothings soothingly into your ear until you fall asleep to the melody of my voice/

I want to feed you sweet fruit, just to watch the motion of your lips and tongue, slowly yet anxiously indulging in the moistness/

I love you from the smell of your hair, to the heartiness of your laugh, to the rhythm in your walk...

... the sly way you smirk, when you're lying or embarrassed or the subtle way your brows turn up when you're pissed off...

I'm captivated by every motion, every feeling, every feature, and everything that makes you you.

My heart flutters when you sneak behind me and wrap your arms comfortably but securely around my waist, gently placing your head on my shoulder, softly kissing my cheek...in that moment in time my world is in one accord/

I love the way you stroke my stomach when I'm deep in contemplation or the way you bite your lip when we indulge in deep conversation/

I can't help but daydream about you throughout my day, I see your image everywhere I go/

You capture my heart, my mind, my body, and my soul...you're my lover, my friend, my counselor, my everything...

My *song cry*, my *sexy love*, my *irreplaceable*, my *incomplete*, and *my boo*/

You complete me like a jigsaw puzzle, making each piece of me fit together perfectly/

When I'm with you, it's as if nothing else matters
and cloud nine is ours forever/

I crave your sweet passion like a newborn yearns for warm milk/

My affection is as natural as the earth, and as genuine
as a white diamond/

I don't wish to bore you with my adoration nor overwhelm you with my desire, but your love is so intoxicating, you could make poison a delectability/

You are my intimate bliss, my very first kiss, my one true love, who I will forever miss...you are the love of my life, the better half of me/

Saying life would be incomplete without you is an understatement, simply because you are life...

You're every breath I take, every move I make...and that's why my life's at stake every time we say goodbye/

Love, you're in every word I speak, every thought I think, every image I see, baby you're all of me…

…and I are you and we are two, inseparable, compatible, and undeniable forces of a boundless bond/

How can our love be so natural, and yet so surreal/

Remember the time when we first met, when we first fell in love, when we first disagreed, when we first broke up, and when we first made up.

...I know you remember making up, because it was like falling in love together... all-over-again...

August 8, 2007

Caught Up (A Spoken Word Piece)

Aye Love, do me this justice by justly answering me this modest question…

Say Love, don't misinterpret this sincerity, in jest of this unapologetic message/

Hold on, before you make blame, and take offense,
don't get the wrong impression…/

So quick to claim defense, though I do need
a genuinely clear answer/

Real talk, never mind the silly mind games, trust, this is no trivial lesson/

Sped Up*

And yes I'd much prefer an honest solution…you know,
minus the bullshit confusion/

Past the intro illusions, so that finally, finally…
we can get to a concrete conclusion.../

So before you cock back your neck and sigh…
before you bite your tongue, roll your eyes…

…and offensively began to imply...the worst... ***pause***

Stop, think deeply first ***pause, exhale****…
then allow me a heartfelt reply...

But on some real type ish, on some *Montel, Dr. Phil* type ish,
"Did you *eva*' care about me?"/

"Did you wake up each and every morning, contemplating,
'Where we would be?'" /

If this "us" simply never was and fallin' in love
was just fabricated; a silly dream"…

Crazy as it seems…

All I ask is that you consider these major facts,
and relieve me of this lust/

Cuz' we both know deep down there was never any fa real' trust/

So don't deny me internal sanctity, and at least respect me
enough with the decency of a excuse/

Cuz' I'm sick and tired of the emotional abuse, and I'm hot and
bothered from your careless misuse…of this impressionable red
muscle that once upon a time extracted susceptible feelings of
passions in fashions so profuse/

But does it make me any better because I don't deny it/

Because instead of running away, I choose to fight it/

Cuz my conscience is weary of chronic lies,
body dreary from tonic fights/

Still, you were my guilty pleasure, my "pick me up"
wherever, whenever…

My best kept secret…honored you like no other,
my intimate, distant lover…/
My endless fantasy, you provoked hopeful realities/

Evoked chokehold formalities…denoted enduring casualties/
Promoted alluring brutalities of love-hate tragedies/
Postponed the relevant and necessary apologies…/
Prolonged arguments in consequential actualities…/

Reminiscin' the thought of us has caused me
some abrupt sickness/
Head thumpin', stomach churning, throat itchy, slightly burning/
Thoughts twisted, word's unlisted, conscience unfitted,
body shifted/
Then I pause to think, what the hell makes the difference?/
I talk, you listen, you talk, but never finish/
Both of us eccentric…both caught in lust, lost in transition/
Sometimes I think I miss it, then I playback,
rewind that decision/

Exhale

So really, I think this shit is kinda' silly/
And I know you think I'm kinda' crazy, but you must admit
you're kinda' shady/
…and baby you can't relay the fact that as far as this engage-
ment, you've been more than kinda' lazy/
…and I know you're thinkin' "is she kinda' playin?",
Cuz I can already hear you sayin', "what did I do, I'm good,
always cool,…"/
…while I just sit back mellow-smooth with a bluntly, sarcastic
attitude…like…
"Yeah, you right boo"…/

"Yeah, it was never you, you were never in the wrong, you have
nothing to feel sorry for because you're perfect and I'm the one
who should hold my tongue."/
"Sure, I deserve your bullshit, yeah I'm the fool, yeah you got it,
yeah you were always good, always cool…"

But then again…who knows…. ***pause***

Maybe you're just a phase, just a "lesson of the day," just another lover, another "bay"/

…and maybe it wasn't meant to be, but then again maybe I needed you just as much as you needed me/

But weren't we at least friends,
at least that was my impression boo/

Somewhere love went sour, started arguing
more than laughin' with you/

It's funny how we'd debate over the pettiest little things, it's funny how I even considered "happily ever after"
and symbolic rings…/

Part of me wishes that all of this was a just dream, and that I never requested your presence and that the essence of my life would still be redeemed/

Then the other half of me thanks you for your laugh, for your smile…for the accent, for the times, for the little while,
which we shared/

Nothing compares to that connection, those late night sessions, but now it's no longer relevant, it's no longer evident, that which was then is no longer now, and what was once is no longer endowed…a bond we had found…now lost, out of touch, out of sound… ***pause***

Like Benjamin André, I apologize, if this message gets you down, but…/

I laugh at myself, thinking how all this occurred,
this brief annihilation of what coulda been, shoulda been,
woulda been relationship, now deterred…

Where did it all go wrong, when did it all fall down, how many apologies and "my bads" can we go year round?…. /

Basically, this shit is getting old, this merry-go-around of a friendship is tired and distressing and I'm simply over pressing what's depressing you and pleading if there's anything that I can do, because… there isn't…cause your heart's choice is solely up to you./

And I'm simply up to the here, of you…so the only option I have is to fall back, recollect my thoughts and mentally get rid of you/ get my mind back on track, reevaluate my life, cool off
and just relax…./

Then, yet again, weren't we friends, weren't we close, what started out as a friendly joke is now a friendless hope, a kinship now eloped…I wanted deeply to be your dope, but just ended up being your "dope," ***laughing****…./

A fool for you, of course, but I'm no fool, foolish maybe, but you pretend like all this makes no sense, like I'm crazy…
but then again I must be… ***pausing, thinking****/

Who else would wholeheartedly give up half their time, an unhealthy portion of their good mind, just to get a quarter of a warm smile….out of you? ***questionable tone**** /

Yeah I *must* be insane, *must* be the blame, *must* be the one who needs to change./

Had to be out of my good mind to think you actually cared,
to think you felt at all…

Silly me… fooled myself there. ***smiling****/

Thought we were having a ball, never doubted that
you would always call/

Never asked myself what I did wrong. /

Why I deserved to be neglected, to be dismissed/

Disrespected like an irrelevant, malevolent,
loveless piece of shit…/

But I can already picture your face, turned up, inside out/

Like, "what the f— is she talking about?"/

As if I'm making this bullshit up, to get a laugh, to get sympathy, to get in one last fight/

Because I'm an over emotional, over sensitive,
over dramatic lame, right? /

You got it, if that's what helps your conscience,
if that's how you sleep at night. /

Then believe what you must, but love ***emphasize*** trust when I say…
you felt it… you felt me… you felt us…just like you feel this…you
can lie to me but not internally…to yourself…/

Ultimately…sucks to be **caught up**….

December 23, 2007

B@ck2Re@lity

Dark and grimly lit, watching the clouds share a kiss
grey and foggy mists overshadow the early morning sky
December chills, bring about sudden frills,
persists the cool air breeze, as the sun starts to rise
dreaming of distant lovers, missing long lost others,
reminiscing of constant loving, dwelling on absent touches
breathing in slow and deep, exhaling softly, pausing to think...
inhaling life in all its glory, all its beauty…
eyes teary from the harsh wind breeze
heart stark, deeply rooted like great oak trees
mind fading, lost in thought, lost in translation,
drifting off like wild tides of ocean seas.
Running wild beyond sugar fields, overcome by sweetness,
drowning in miles and miles of bliss…
racing against cupid's bow and arrow, hit or miss
running blindly, fighting the cold air, as the evening sun approaches
face taking a break, kneeling to give thanks an say grace.
For you, for a new day, for new life, for new love and a new way
returning to my run, sprinting all the way back home
back to reality, back to life and back to love where I belong...

June 10, 2011

Poison

The smoothest preacher a set his morals aside if the right one came along/Devil in a blue dress,

Sweet as first kisses—-swags no contest, venom in em'
like a Middle Eastern viper/

Swipe your good heart and right mind, Spray souls with passion steel 9s-her looks kill better than trained militia sniper frontlines...

Sincerely,
~ Jai

P.S. Desire,

I pray that one day you allow yourself to experience, pursue and prosper in the real thing, without hesitation, without procrastination and essentially without fear—for you are truly an original. Although that "too cool for school" attitude might be advantageous to your artful lifestyle and endeavors of edgy fashion, raw music and strange clouds now, love there is so much more to life than the façade and campaign of sex, drugs and rock and roll.

When we were connected I always sensed a sentimental depth of potential in you that struggled so desperately to erupt and shed that emotional layer of ascetic, rhino skin you swagged so effortlessly. Because believe it or not Desire, despite your suppressed past, your domestic pain and growing up spoiled beyond reason, you do deserve to be happy; and not the happiness our pop culture perceives on television or in the magazines but the head over heels, reach for the stars, late night to early morning-no words-just breathing on the phone-type happiness we dreamed of way back when we were teens; because in the end ALL that will matter is that YOU loved.

A renowned social psychologist Leonard Berkowitz cited "that if we could overcome our inhibitions and show our emotions , we would eliminate disturbing tensions, conquer nagging aches and pains and promote "deeper" and "more meaningful" relationships with others"... ***sighs***... Amen.

We come to love not by finding a perfect person,

but by learning to see an imperfect person perfectly.

~ Sam Keen

II.

"GUILTY PLEASURE" *(Lust)*

Soundtracks "Say Yes" - Floetry |
"Stingy" - Ginuwine |
"Next Lifetime" - Erykah Badu |

Quote *"You can close your eyes*
to the things you do not want to see,
but you cannot close your heart
to the things you do not want to feel."

~ Tabitha Suzuma

Dear Lust,

(Fall)

Lust is a funny thing…it's like a generic love, a fabricated passion and an illusive connection; and too often what happens is initially we fail to distinguish its facade from *love*…until of course it ends. You were indeed one of the first friends whose relationship I wish remained platonic. We were so blindly selfish in our infidelity that we couldn't even recognize it as an affair.

Looking back, you and I began so unintended yet felt inextricably emphatic and disturbingly purposeful. When we first met I fell into a courtship with your childhood friend who was introduced with intent for us to date by your lover at the time who was also a very good friend of mine. I looked up to your lover like an older cousin who looked after me like a kid sister. To this day if it's one thing I regret, and I never regret, it's my disloyalty to her and our kinship.

I mean it didn't matter that she was no good for you or that you both *stepped out* on each other religiously but it wasn't my place to judge or fix; and as my friendly relational advice to you turned into friendly sympathy outings and flirtations—it seemed as though between my denial and self-regarding cupidity and your gluttony for attention we were living a lie of lust, deceit and betrayal.

Sure our closest friends encouraged the affair because they witnessed the happiness it brought us despite its undeniable iniquity. But I think what ultimately kept us from ending was our dynamic friendship and our desire for something better. You cheated because of the neglect you experienced in your long-distance relationship to one of my good college friends. I allowed you to cheat because I knew that good friend was, did and would always cheat on you despite the affinitive history that you both shared. But it got to a point where that excuse no longer held weight and my guilt and karmic conscience began eating away at my spirit.

It had to hit me the night your childhood friend who, enraged, sent my roommate and best friend a yahoo instant message saying how hurt your lover and my good friend were by our affair and how everyone around us (i.e, our close friends) pretended like it was acceptable to engage in. For the first time since we began pursuing this lust I felt a sense of unbearable shame and disgrace that drowned my spirits so deep that I wanted to flee to a dark corner and hide. While my sister assured me it was unnecessary dramatics and you brushed it off as competitive envy and pride from your childhood friend losing me to you, but I knew different, I knew better; and I knew that despite her motives, that she was right…and what we were doing was undoubtedly wrong, no excuses, no justifications. I was convinced from that day on that it had to end; we had to end. Despite the infidelity and neglect from your lover and my yearning to rescue and lead you into a better relationship it wasn't my place to interfere.

So days later, following threats and provocations from both your lover and childhood friend of how boldly immoral we were to carry on as lovebirds as if we were both unattached, I made up my mind that enough was enough and this isn't what or who I wanted to be or remembered for. As much as I loved you even though I wasn't in love, my soul knew it wasn't true and because of that it became lust. The day I ended it I recall you simply starring at me out of scrutiny as if you didn't understand why or how we couldn't continue our relationship. It was then that you were so caught up in a remorseless, self-fulfilling capacity that it became quite clear to me that you never saw a problem with what we were doing and if I permitted us to continue that you never would. Immediately upon our demise I felt a weight lifted off my shoulders, and though I could physically see how much it hurt you I knew it was the right thing and prayed to God He would spare me future karmic consequences.

August 1, 2008

It's All in Love

You know I care about you right, you know it's all love,
When we swear, when we fight
You push and shove but I know it's not in spite
Distant love, forget me not another night...
Close your eyes relax and breathe
Mesmerized in lust, new feelings I fear I've conceived
Developed trust, tell me true love do you believe
Or have you abandoned love, because of lies and deceit
Pity the soul whose heart is put on lease
Feel for them for love to them is now buried and deceased
Let love decide your fate, live everyday like loves the last
Chance, your last break…promise, my mind you won't fake,
Promise my heart you won't break,
Promise, my love you won't forsake....

August 8, 2008

The Art of Seduction

Sweet, inescapable, mellow smooth
Sensually, arousing as intimate love tunes
Tantalizing sweets, attract even the bitterest fools
Succumbed to tasteful lovers, overpowered
by lust's delectable rules
illustrious design of pure perfection
Exalted in beauty, scorned by preference
visual too deep, intense and yet so meek
souls attract, collapse, then peak to cognitive erections
lost in love's experimentations with promiscuous temptations,
I nominate you yes you, in these trials,
guaranteed this love's election...
...my soul candidate, we contrast
as black and white like keys on a piano...
soft strokes replace light taps,
composing enticing notes never played never heard
Two bodies melt into one, grinding, slowly submerged,
rapid circular motions gradually occur without
impassioned three letter words
coming together to
create this musical, visual masterpiece, vivid emotions deterred
Solely moaning sounds of warm, flesh-pounding hues heard
electrifying, heart-firing and body wiring like
Breath-taking Van Goghs, seductive Beethovens,
And erotic Michangelos toss and turned...when we make art....

August 9, 2008

Techno Nympho

Melodic notes extract smooth metaphors and anecdotes
Impact beautiful minds, soothe genius bodies,
and surpass infinite times
Illustrate eloquent rhymes, speaking complex portraits,
priceless masterpieces,

All one of a kind
Endless dreams provoke hopeful realities
Evoke chokehold formalities
Denote enduring causalities
Promote alluring brutalities of love hate tragedies
Postpone the apologies
Skip the process, just marry me
Prolong the intimate technology of virtual love
Cyber kisses and hugs, touch that key that makes me plead
Sensual messages that shake me weak
Unexpected aims that cause thoughts to peak
Away me I beg, so that only then I can be sent to sleep...

September 22, 2008

Invisible Tears

You left your gentle scent lingering between the cool creases
of my soft sheets
Warm aromas of cherry blossom fragrance wrapped softly
around my pillows, sugary sweet
You kissed me goodbye but I didn't return the passion
Side tracked by the thought of you leaving me,
leaving us behind quickly fastened
Holding you tight, gripping your waist, avoiding the deep
sadness in your face, and in your eyes
Both of us staring off into space, into the night,
reminiscing of the time that past, dismissing desired cries
Holding back those deep streams of water that persist in falling
down your brown cheeks
Stubborn, you resist, but I feel your strength
and want you to let go, and finally give in to me
...so then I can wipe away your waterfalls,
and rescue you from your deeply hidden pain
One last kiss, one long kiss goodnight I unwillingly submit,
for your lips I can't refrain
Holding back the passion, realizing the moment is just that,
"a moment;"

once again I try and restrain
Released from your embrace, I struggle,
slowly, coldly walking away
Careful not to return, not to say those three little words
that make everything all okay
Fighting not to turn around and yell for you to wait,
fighting not to look back, I continue to walk astray,
head high, fists tight, lips numb and cold…
Caught up in mixed emotions, parts untouched and words untold
Hopelessly lost in deep thought, suddenly overcome
by random fears, awaiting love's heartbreak,
drowning in our invisible tears...

September 28, 2008

Confession

Love me, love me not, miss me, forget me not
Weary from constant pretending, tired of faking friendly,
when deep down, I'd much prefer late night sessions
of whole hearted confessions of how much of a
Blessing it is to share the pure essence of your warm presence
Making eye contact, my heart flutters
Words stutter, thoughts jumble, feet stumble,
an utter catastrophe every time we speak
Feelings suddenly reoccur like it's the very first time
that we meet
Most nights I imagine you're never alone
At least not physically, but emotionally I can see
That your heart is single, unattached and without security
Naturally you seek a rare love with whom to be
Only if you'd give me the time of day,
then could I rescue you from loveless misery

October 1, 2008

Cupid's Fool

I'm the type who always wants what they can't get,
and always gets what they don't want...
"Hard to get" is a game much preferred
Even if in the midst emotions stir
Then chemistry persists and stomachs churn
If I can't have all of you then I'd rather have no part
Sike naw, I'd take you in any shape or form...
if you'd let me in at all
Even if you gave in I'd hesitate, unsure of where to start and how
If love is a game for fools then I fear I'm playing by your rules
But now I must choose, either move on or be that fool
Crushed like a love struck school girl, I'm throwed
Letting go like Keyshia Cole, you bluffed me once,
game over, time to fold
Hearts done racing, no more
Chasing, silly love, you're my replacement…

October 10, 2008

Jokes on Me

Folk you a joke really thought you had it in the bag huh
Pass the asthma pump, because you choked
and lost what you never had
Wipe the egg off ya face, because you neva was
gettin any face, anyway
Yea you got punked, sent ya fast tail on a wild ahh goose chase
But as the movie reaches its climax, you set to a pause
And it's far too late to slow down now...
Bet you wish you could rewind back now
It's like you trapped in a horror flick, or maybe a bad dream
And this one comes with a sad ending
and your feelings you can't redeem
I laugh at the hurt because "I told you so" was too damn easy
Shoulda listened to your conscience now you're a victim

of your own teasing
Boo came with a pre-posted warning label
but you were still tempted to tear the wrapper
Now look at you, full of resentment and desperate
to return the package
Stuck with this tainted feeling but it's as useless
as soiled napkins
Now you staring at your reflection,
looking back at yourself like damn, what happened?
So what to do when you're lost, so confused,
caught up in the game
Trapped in lust, in chase of something
and someone you never once had claim...

October 17, 2008

Guilty Pleasure (Sweet Escape)

The sweetest risk, something like my guilty pleasure
my distant, secret lover...however, whenever, wherever
if loving you is wrong, damn I don't wanna be right
if loving you is just a dream, I can't wait until the night
like an unwrapped gift I selfishly keep you all to me
careful not to let people touch or hold you,
because some are just unworthy
Though you're not fully mine, I know a part of me
will always be close to your heart
I mean as long as you know how I feel I know
we'll never grow far apart
you know that unconditional love...
that priceless, can't eat, can't sleep,
thank the man above type love
my nicotine, my Luther's house without home, my ecstasy,
my Monica's so gone
my late night energy boost, my morning caffeine
my addiction, my natural high,
something like a recovering love fiend
if lovin' you is wrong, this is my silent confession

forgive me for this lustful sin, rid me of this forsaken passion
afraid to lose you, love I'd never refuse you
you haunt my thoughts, daydreams and fantasies all the daylong
your smile, your lips, your eyes, all stuck in my head
like my favorite love song
some feel like we're not meant to be; if they only knew
that love can't discriminate, so neither should we
of course they hate, they doubt, they question;
well I say let us be their first love's lesson
Love like this is fearless, exceeding all bounds and levels
I could never deny you love, my sweet escape,
my lovable, guilty pleasure...

October 21, 2008

R.I.P. L.O.V.E

The day she died I broke down and cried
tossin' and turnin', voice shot, mouth dried
Tears raining down my face, throat on fire,
yelling until I got tired
Struggling back and forth, caught in a tug of war emotion
Losing this lust driven battle of chaotic
desires stirring up passionate commotion
and yet I grieve alone for the only one who could console me
is now forever gone
left me without warning, I sat waiting for your sweet
good morning but little did I know,
that'd be your last sweet good morning,
now I sit by the window and stare, dazed and mourning
Dreaming of how to bring you back to life and back to me
but all I can do is ask why?
Why did you leave, why you and not me,
how we ever came to be
and why one day you'd have to leave me behind
in loveless misery
The day love died, I laid down and cried...
that faithful day I lost my mind, lost direction, then lost time...

...an sadly with her, a piece of me also became deceased...

October 24, 2008

Bandit Called Love

Not going out because my heart aches, mind half baked,
not much more can I take...
and my head's thumping, my stomach's churning,
throat's burning
my thoughts are twisted and my words unlisted,
what's the difference, I talk you listen, you talk but don't finish,
both of us eccentric, both lost in transition,
I hope that you miss me, my dope, be my addiction,
we grow and I envision a life with you I'm missing...
your faults are my strengths and you have no reason
to feel shamed because we all make mistakes,
forgive me for any pain brought upon, for that I am ashamed,
for being insincere, for listening to whispers in my ear,
versus my heart,
I owe that much my dear, but you fooled me
and I reacted harshly, straight off emotion,
I stumbled and lost focus, but fear not because I'm refocused,
smile so I can begin to re-open, my heart
because now it's broken, how do we start
to get back in motion, oh love make me whole again...
I'm lost, heart stolen.

November 1, 2008

Lust

With you being bad never felt so good
You make me say things I never thought I would
You make me do things I never felt I should
You make me feel ways I never dreamed I could
The essence of your presence is so deep
I lose myself when I see you, on instant I become weak

You do something to me, others just can't see
You slow and speed up my heart all at the same time,
never missing a beat
You give off this mystic vibe like
it's almost impossible not to feel you
My attraction is almost forced like I can't help myself
but to want you
I fear my feelings aren't mutual but even worst
I feel like they're dismissed
This temptation's fatal to my mind, heart, every single bit
I just don't know how much more I can handle of this lust s—.

November 13, 2008

Careless

She's careless, she's heartless...she's lost and she's bothered
caught up, looking back, tracing facts at what caused this
fighting her feelings, careful not to let emotions
overpower her intelligence
paranoia sets in when the whispers in her ear come in,
yet she knows it's irrelevant
but no worries my dear, she doesn't care
because she has nothing to fear
she doesn't bleed nor sweat, nor cry, no tears...
heart made out of stone, just an icebox there but don't fret,
for you know love's unfair or did you forget because now
everything's so clear
moment of clarity, seeing the light for the first time
like I'm up from a deep sleep
In a trance, waiting for my last chance, no last dance,
I'm drained, body too weak
hearts blown, mind gone, spirits so strong, for feelings to share
guess that's why "love" I don't fear, guess that's why I'm free,
heart clear because I always make myself believe I can't care...

November 30, 2008

Rescue Me

Who rescues the invincible superman from his kryptonite?
Who saves us from invisible tears
we work so hard to hold, to fight?
Who protects the lone heroes in their weak state?
We hear your cries, race to your side, and never hesitate
Accept your pleas and honor your deepest trust
In them you confide your fears, your pain, even your lust
But who mourns for the selfless hero, who fights for the champ
Who gives their last breath to the lifesaver,
who cries for the child inside the man?
Who holds her hand when she's the one lost and scared
Who rebuilds her up as she's left open, broken and bare
Who looks out for her heart when she's healed
so many in silent pleas?
Who returns the favor of the Good Samaritan's deed?
Who loves the friend who's always loved you more than a friend
Who rescues the hero when it's them
who need someone in which to love and depend...?

Sincerely,
~ Jai

P.S. Lust,

As you know you were my first and that is something and someone special you can never really forget. ***laughing***...when we first learn about intimacy, most of us tend to imagine it as something brilliantly and extravagantly orchestrated at the right place at the perfect time. But we're never ready, it's never the best time and as far as the illustrious design and aura of sensual ambiances and decadent décor and whatnot, it's as surreal as the intensity we hope to experience.

Nevertheless, in these instances your pleasure has always been the beneficiary of my own so at the satisfactory gestures, sounds and response that you shared, I can confidently say it was successful to say the least. Not only were you the "first" but you were also the first person I deeply cared for who reciprocated those exact feelings and that's most likely what kept me intrigued in our blasphemous rendezvous. I was 19 and all I saw and all I wanted was you and that selfishness absorbed my better judgment as we all sometimes fall victim to especially at that age. We were one of those situations where in maturing you begin to realize that sometimes your personal decisions have an effect on more than just you. It was the first time I felt wholly and inescapably guilty and ashamed of what I chose to indulge in and from that instance on I vowed to abstain from involving myself in another couple's relationship no matter the temptation, separation or justification. It just wasn't me or what I aspired to have.

In the years that passed I often tried to rekindle our friendship but soon realized that the emotions stirred from the facade of rejection you believe I left you with was far too ineffable for us to mend even as friends. After some months I learned you were pregnant and dating someone I knew, which surprisingly didn't bother me as much as I thought, seeing how the pregnancy overlapped with the time we were dating. Truthfully, it made sense that you would be cheating on your mistress while your lover cheated on you. Come to find, the father of your child would leave you for another woman whom he would also impregnate, marry and then leave as well, in which all awhile you would remain in the long-distance relationship with the initial lover you had stepped out on with me. It became one of those situations that though I sympathized for I still shook my head and thanked God he freed me of that emotive rollercoaster before the ride got too real.

Last I heard your baby girl was healthy, growing up and you were enlisted in the military reserves, working and maintaining a happy relationship with a new man in your life. About a year ago I had the pleasure of seeing you and your family up close on a random errand run to the local grocery store. I recognized you but avoided eye contact because I honestly wasn't prepared to speak or acknowledge your presence. Yes, it was immature and ridiculous but at the time I was just content seeing that you were happy with your new family from afar. A part of me believes you saw me as well and maybe out of discomfort or unexplained disorientation (like I) that you simply pretended you hadn't. It was then that I felt a nostalgic flush of peace hoping to God it was as good as it seemed and that one day He'd grant me the same karmic mercy and grace.

To love is to risk not being loved in return. To hope is to risk pain. To try is to risk failure, but risk must be taken because the greatest hazard in life is to risk nothing.

~ Leo F. Buscaglia

III.

"FIRST LOVE" *(Mi Amor)*

Soundtracks "Song for You" - Donnie Hathaway |
"Can't Be Friends" - Trey Songz |
"Someone Like You" - Adele |

Quote *"There is never a time or place for true love. It happens accidentally, in a heartbeat, in a single flashing, throbbing moment."*

~ Sarah Dessen

Dear Mi Amor,

(Spring)

Remember that feeling when your heart beat fast and slow at the same time and when it pounded so loud and hard it felt like it was pumping outside of your rib cage. Remember when our emotions were so ablaze that we felt pain and pleasure all in the same motion... and our world stopped and stood still, causing our thoughts to blur. Remember how your feet seemed light as a feather as if you were walking on air, floating in space and time... Love, the greatest emotion known to man...can make you feel low, make you feel high, make you feel weak, make you feel strong, make you feel wise, ***laughing*** make you feel crazy, but most importantly it makes you feel LOVE…that is exactly how my love was for you, my first love.

Well, it seems to me that the best relationships—the ones that last—are frequently the ones that are rooted in friendship. You know, one day you look at the person and you see something more than you did the night before. Like a switch has been flicked somewhere; and the person who was just a friend is... suddenly the only person you can ever imagine yourself with.

~ Gillian Anderson.

As beautiful spring approached at the end of our sophomore year in college, the flowers weren't the only thing blooming a new season. On April 15, 2009, for the first time in my life I shared my heart with another being and hopelessly fell in love with you, one of my best friends. That bless'ed date marked a day of surrealism I would never forget for as long as I live, a day that would later become our first anniversary. Little did I know… two years later you would let me go, break my heart and in turn set me free.

In so many words, my first love and our relationship ended because you felt morally and spiritually imbalanced, as you once described it. You classified yourself as a straight woman and though you fell in love you felt that our lifestyle wasn't ultimately what you wanted or who you were; and so you opted to end our relationship, indulge in your singlehood and begin publicly dating the one person my woman's intuition always presumed you were "involved" with from jump. We were together for one year and six months.

In everything that we had been through and all the critics and haters that we proved wrong and put to shame; the friends we inspired to take emotive risks, give into their heart's desires and even to fall in love—we were unintentionally the poster-couple for true love, straight, bi, gay or otherwise. We were what people strived for.

You, being my first and longest love and confidant, I can't help but think how we made promises and were always there for each other. I was there when your beloved younger cousin passed away even though we were miles apart. I was there when the recession and FASFA threatened your college graduation and almost imposed on us a long-distance relationship. And I was there to build you up when your mother's verbal trample over your mental and emotional self-esteem almost broke you down. I was there. And you were too. When I tried to hide the pain of knowing my sister was moving away for good, you were there to rid me of my insensitive attitude, expose me for my selfishness and possibly save our friendship. Your expressed disappointment in my selfish behavior practically brought me to shame and in turn helped me realize what I almost lost—a good friend...and yet ‘til this day I still have my sister but not you. Where are you now?....

May 11, 2009

First Love Letter

Life is but a dream/having you here with me/kissing you endlessly/loving so carelessly/daybreak to sunset we lay together overcome by deep touches and cognitive pulses/stirred by stimulant conversing heightening the loving.... again and again and again...*to be continued.*

May 12, 2009

Cognitive Utopia

As we journey through cultivated paths of experiences, emotions, thoughts and hazy expectations, in the midst we’re met with an unpredictable bliss, our private utopias engulfed in our natural schemas...set in a world which we create in our memories, a dimension beyond thy human imagination...a mentality solely gained through our subconscious...it is in this place where hearts race minds coast and spirits collide, where we discover the ideals of our existence; here we search for meaning and understanding, here we cease to judge and increase the effort to learn... this is where love is created and embraced...where rules of society diminish and truth and faith are the only resorts to ultimate freedom happiness and peace overall, thy humanitarian dream and mine for you and me...

December 31, 2009 (11:59 pm)

Dear Mi Amor,

I wanted to be your first New Year's Day message…First of all I just want to thank you for sharing this gracious year with me through the good and bad...Lord knows I wouldn't have made it without Him and your support. You changed my life in so many ways for the good and everyday we're together I feel like a better person...I have so much to be thankful for this year and I can honestly say I have you to thank for that because you play such a major part in my life and 09' was our year, baby...I didn't imagine falling in love like this at 20 years of life but I know that this was the right time the perfect time and God's time for us to be united like we are despite what the world thinks because all that matters is what's true to your heart and my heart is only true with you...

Blessings to you and your family and I pray that 2010 will bring us endless joy and faith..."ily" always and forever bay I feel that we can only get better only come closer and only love harder with time...I've loved before you and I will love after you but I will never love another the way that I love you...you are my true love, love, your #1 fan....

May 18, 2009

Dear Mi Amor,

Let it rain, let it rain...quiet showers against my window pane. Rapid drip drops cause my heart to flip flop, churns my stomach making it flutter. Swirling endlessly like the wind outside, emotional butterflies forcing me to smile...and all the while all the while I think of you, Mi Amor... almond eyes alluring and calming like the drizzle pouring from the sky...your gaze soft yet bold calling me near like hypnosis, I'm taken away caught up in your heavenly portrait. Like the rain your love is a Godsend, so natural but so very rare...wishing ever so deeply that you could rock me to sleep like the peaceful rain near me...

May 20, 2009

Wakin' Up

Wakin' up I exhale out loud, thank God I'm alive
Thank God for sound mind
Dreamin' of you last night
Reminiscin' somethin' distant,
Laughin' off that Color Purple tip, "all my life I had to fight"…
Mesmerized, I fantasize of better days and deeper ways to
express myself
… and profess what's left….
Contemplating what it is that I want, what it is that I need,
When really it's love, true love which we creates us
into such fiends.
Embellished in bliss, how could one fake
How could one refuse such embrace,
such disgrace is the man who under appreciates his blessings,
his strengths; yet I lie awake, emotions without a trace,
zoned out thoughts lost in outer space
Body limp and out of place, sore from the sweet pain
of immense weight...
And yet I lie awake, free from sunrise wake,
free to roam, free to breathe
Free to indulge in all life's simplicity
However I wait, wait for your return and only then can I truly
rest soundly in your arms…no need to set the alarm. ***wink***

May 25, 2009

My Heart's Hue

Beauty is in the eye of thy beholder... Natural browns and calm blues powdery whites sensual reds soothing yellows potent purples and mellow greens mesh together to create God's Picasso paradise...this utopian dream which for me is and will always be you.

May 27, 2009

How Do You…?

How do you find the one that you dream about?
How do you fall in love carefree no doubts?
How do you know who the one is, if it's real, when to separate the fiction from the surreal...
…the "just enough" from the ideal…
…the can't eat can't sleep, wish upon a star-type feelings;
from the lustful affairs of secular fantasies
of shallow driven physicalities...
Or dealings...of such, not sure of all thy answers
but I know this much.
It's the simple things...a gaze, a smirk, a gesture, a touch...
this is how I know...
…that is how I distinguish love from lust, truth from mirage, destiny from fantasy, fate from irony.
It's simple, if only they could see..that I was made for you and you were made for me...my dream come true, Mi Amor always and forever we shall be...from irony….

May 28, 2009

Our Piece of Heaven

Warms my heart thinking about how good we felt how safe, real and natural everything became...I never took us just lying around in each other's arms for granted, it was our little piece of heaven if only for five minutes before work or five minutes after class started... I was at peace knowing just for that moment nothing and no one else mattered...not school not track not money not the drama...just me an Mi Amor...those moments those fragments those getaways from the world outside you and me were stepping stones to falling in an unthinkable love deeper than the imagination, better than them and bigger than us....

May 31, 2009

Dear Mi Amor,

In case you didn't know you're my best friend...I have sisters, cousins and close friends with whom I love and who love me but none of those relationships compare to the bond we share. No matter what happens between us you will always be the person I want to talk to when I first wake up to the time I fall asleep. I can share anything with you and I trust you with my heart and soul. I'm most vulnerable with you because it's to the point where you know me inside and out; my flaws, my ups and downs, what makes me tick and for that you are my better part.

June 1, 2009

Highs & Lows

Through good times and bad, moods change like the seasons.
Searching for logical answers like earth wind and fire reasons.
Feelings succumb as submissive as captive slaves.
Emotions flow endlessly, constant;
and yet as unpredictable as the days.
Up and down, in and out, everyday is a new chance
to express a thought, an emotion.
A chance to regress, impress and progress
in this jungle we call our lives.
Fighting with our identities, our psyches, in these trying times…
Faith and love are the only things keeping us alive...

June 3, 2009

Mind Race

Words in motion, thoughts provoking from distant loving,
long lost others.
Broken promises and wishful thinking...
...thoughts preceding emotions fleeing;
when really internally,
I'm pleading for second chances, eternal romances,
and external glances cause tingly trances;
but reality bites back when I sway too far off track,
in this race of life this striding through love;
careful to pace, breathing deeply I cruise,
controlled and smooth, sprinting to first place.

June 6, 2009

On My Way Home

Black skies secure the night; drift me from a long day,
a long drive home....
Scattered stars watching down soothe me now,
for rest is all I seek.
Silent sounds are all that surround, as the cool air breeze.
Exhale loud, deep breath in, longing hoping,
where does one begin?....
Thoughts racing, practicing patience...I pray that it finds me.
Reminiscing, dreaming awake and remembering why I smile.
Searching within I recall again that love that drives me wild.
Never leaving, never fleeing your heart remains inside,
My soul my mind my spirit it resides,
which makes the journey worthwhile.
On my way home again, against the cold past, I surrender.
In midst of the dark I remain at peace for my memory sedates me
so now pressure is ceased.
No stress no pain no ache no shame.
Just hope and faith of new life, a new day...

on my way coming home……these thoughts,
your inspiration keeps me sane and never alone.

June 8, 2009

Make You Feel

That feeling when your heart beats fast and slow
at the same time.
When your heart pounds so loud and hard
it feels like it's beating through your rib cage.
When your emotions are so ablaze that you feel
pain and pleasure all in the same wave...
…your world stands still and your thoughts begin to cave…
your feet are light as a feather and it's as if you're walking on air,
floating in time....
Love, the greatest feeling known to man...
make you feel low, make you feel high,
make you feel weak, make you feel strong, make you feel wise,
make you feel crazy, make you feel captive, make you feel wild
but most importantly... it makes you "feel"...

June 9, 2009

Whisper low kiss me slow touch so light smile so slight...this is how your love captures me from early sunrise to deep in the night...**Morning, Mi Amor.**

June 10, 2009

Dear Jai,

It's crazy how you and I came to be, all I know is I just can't stop thinking, breathing, wondering about you, "you got me straight trippin' boo" hehe. All jokes aside Jai, I hope you resting well honey bunches of caramel...oooohhh that sweet tangy sugar honey ice tea, that warms and soothes my mind body and soul all because of the secret ingredient you added to it from the inner self, which mirrors your true beauty and as you lay your body next to mine, both our spirits are calm, soothed, relaxed but deeply perplexed about how and why God himself allowed this be…to BE strong, BE loving BE kind BE cute BE funny BE my sunshine, BE the BEST I EVER HAD... until we get up above, beyond the earthly cloud nine into the streets of heavenly gold....

Yours truly,
Mi Amor

June 10, 2009

Fools in Love

Why do fools fall in love
Why do birds sing
Why are angels sent from above
Why is the earth green
Why does the wind blow
Why is skin so soft
Why does water simply flow
Why is humanity so lost
Why don't we live free
Instead of just existing
Why not embrace presently
Instead of what's missing
Why do we argue
and not compromise
Why is it we want, want, want…
But never sacrifice
Why are the days so long and nights too short
Why is reality so clear but dreams distort
Why do I choose to love you even when I know it might hurt
Because deep down inside I believe I can always make it work...

June 12, 2009

The Way You Make Love Feel

You are the blush in my cheeks,
The thump in my chest that makes my hands tremble,
my knees weak
Even the smirk in my smile
...the chills through my skin,
Tingly sensations have no end and just the mention of your name
drives me wild...
You're the butterflies in my belly,
The pep in my step, the shining glow all throughout my face...
The glitter in my eyes, not even I could hold back a smile
...and so for you I always give thanks...

June 13, 2009

Dear Mi Amor,

Reminiscing of our past, fantasizing about our present and daydreaming of our future are the only things that keep me grounded when we are apart...

June 15, 2009 *(Happy 20th Birthday)*

Dear Mi Amor,

First, I want to thank God for blessing you
with 20 beautiful years of life...
Second I want to thank your parents for creating and raising one
of the strongest most intelligent and attractive individuals
I know...and finally I want to thank you for simply being you...
for being loving, genuine and passionate you.
You are unique beyond words and beyond poetry beyond song...
from head to toe, inside and out and for that I am honored to be
your friend, lover and confidant...
Even though we're apart I still feel your love thousands of miles
away because our connection is ineffable and impenetrable

meaning no one and no circumstance can stop us except for God himself, and I even imagine we're too happy for Him
to allow this to come to an end...
So on your special day I want nothing else but for you to celebrate these last two decades and spend every moment of every second of your best day in bliss and not allow anyone
or anything to ruin that...
I love you and I pray that you'll embrace the day for what it is, a true blessing for you, for your family, as well as for me...
because you are truly a gift, our gift from God....

June 16, 2009

1,065 Miles Away…

Your love carries me
1065 miles away
Your mind seduces me
1065 miles away
Your courage inspires me
1065 miles away
Your beauty amazes me
1065 miles away
Your spirit chases me
1065 miles away
Your kindness comforts me
1065 miles away
Our love overwhelms us
1065 miles away...

June 17, 2009

Dear Jai,

I don't know what to say Jai, but I completely understand your older cousins are concerns about our relationship; they are older thus wiser so I see how they can compare their experience to ours. I'm not saying that our situation is the same because we both know very well we are unique. But we are both mature, intellectual females and can handle our own relationship. Nonetheless, I don't need to preach about what they are concerned with because the reality is, this is something you and I have to face together: I'm classified as straight and you as pan [sexual]. Despite these oppositions, you taught me that the heart has no bias, and though this isn't how I planned my life, this is the way it has come to be. I know within my soul that our peculiar connection defies all and will forever keep us close and our bond irreplaceable. It's kind of why I always joke and say how I believe we would have crossed paths eventually, at some point in this lifetime; if not now then in a year, maybe five or ten, etc., because it's felt like that ever since the day I got to know you. I've been drawn to you and could never explain it. You taught me to feel and not think so much and that's part of life....

As I write this I'm holding back tears because there is no other way to express how I love you I can't speak for the future for it's not known and its normal to fear the unknown that's why your older cousins are concerned with your future, and if we are getting too serious or the simplicity of a symbolic ring is cause for fear then shockingly I welcome it because if we make each other happy then we just can't lose; no matter if you are my friend or lover I'll always remain true to you. Believe that no matter what the future brings and please remember that I'm honest with you because I truly care about you Jai....

Yours truly,
Mi Amor

P.S. If you want the promise ring back then you can have it or if you want to return it so you can contribute it to something worthwhile then I support whatever decision you make as I'm sure your cousins do. I don't need a ring to be with you, only you.

May 21, 2010

Dear Mi Amor,

Reminiscing in the shower of this past year of bliss and craziness with you, I thought how fast time flies and how much we've grown and learned together. I also thought of how and when exactly I fell in love for the first time in my life with someone I never imagined I'd be with, but I couldn't pinpoint the exact moment. Soon I realized there was no one moment because each and every day you do or say something that makes me love you more and more; makes me fall deeper and deeper in love without realizing; whether we have a good day or bad. Whether we fight or make love, some way or another my love for you is revived daily. No matter what the day or night brings my love for you never changes never fails. I believe in you and me and that I've always been sure of. You are my first and best love and for that you are infinitely in my heart. You and I are the face of faith….

May 22, 2010

Dear Mi Amor,

'Strength of our love'…It's hard enough to love someone by itself but it's even harder to love someone and have to hide it. But somehow that doesn't pain me because as long as we know what we have is special and honorable I could care less of what anyone else knows or thinks.

The things I do for your love for your heart. You are the sweetest risk and are worth any heartache to come.

May 29, 2010

Dear Mi Amor,

'Always and forever'…feeling you by the ocean tide and under the Miami stars was so peaceful and comforting that I lost all time and space. I thought this might be the last time I get to touch and caress and share fat spicy food with you for a long time lol but I'm thankful for any time God grants us to share our love. I'm so blessed to have you in my life and I want you to know that there's not a day or hour or minute that goes by that you're not on my mind and in my heart. I love you Mi Amor always and forever. Goodnight and sweet dreams...

May 30, 2010

No Matter What

No matter what happens between us
I will always be a part of you and you of me
Our spirits are inclined to intertwine 'til thy end of time
like a perfect melody
With each day I pray that your love keeps me warm and at peace
Your smile your touch your laugh, soothes,
gives me so much trust in life in love
In miracles sent from above
We are a divine creation of God himself; our existence is living proof that real love is out there somewhere….
The perfect imperfection.

June 1, 2010

Sensitive Soul

I am a sensitive soul, beautiful and strong
I sing sad love songs and write passionate life poems
I am a sensitive soul, young but wise beyond my years
I listen and advise loved ones and weaken their fears
I am a sensitive soul, confident and bold

I hold my head up high and yet i cry to tragedy untold
I am a sensitive soul, humble yet soundly brave
I put you first and sacrifice my desires because of my faith
I am a sensitive soul, patient and forgiving
I practice understanding and acceptance of all the living
I am a sensitive soul, sensual and sometimes meek
I croon to Miles Davis, Sade and Maxwell in hopes to fall asleep.

June 3, 2010

Dear Mi Amor,

Loudly then softly over and over again...
I can feel your bittersweet dark chocolate skin when I close my eyes and drift my mind to the time when our lives were simple and free. Weightless and noncomplex, we lay in each other's arms 'til death did us part. Your lips quench my heart's thirst and your touch takes my body to another world. Wrapped up behind you, cradled beneath me or locked in beside me, your love nests are the sweetest most peaceful places on this earth, at least on my earth....

June 13, 2010

Dear Mi Amor,

Without a shadow of a doubt I know that right now you are the only one for me. God has shown us that in so many ways to even deny that we were meant to love each other. You are my best friend and lover and maybe even my soul mate. My family's love for you is only icing on the cake. I hope that you always feel the same way about us and carry our spiritual love in your heart no matter our distance or time apart. Love you always.

June 15, 2010
Dear Mi Amor,

I thank God for our coexistence…

I thank him for giving you life, thus giving me life therefore allowing "us" life. On June 16, 1989 a miracle occurred and on April 15 2009, 20 years later a miracle was re-born. The day you chose me and we fell in love was truly a gift from God. I pray that He feels your spirit with all your heart's desire. No matter what, you're my shining star. Your light fills me up so let it fill you. I love you baby. Happy birthday and blessings on MCAT.

June 18, 2010
Dear Mi Amor,

"Expressions that remind me of us"

1. *When something is missing in your life, it usually turns out to be "someone."* ~ Robert Brault

2. *To know when to go away and when to come closer is the key to any lasting relationship.* ~ Domenico Cieri Estrada

3. *Soul-mates bring out the best in you. They're not perfect but are always perfect for you.* ~ Author Unknown

4. *You can't stop loving or wanting to love because when it's right, it's the best thing in the world.* ~ Keith Sweat

5. *Passion spins around love and I am dizzy always around you.* ***wink*** ~ Albany Bach Reid

June 19, 2010

Dear Mi Amor,

In love you learn to put the other person's needs and wants before your own; yet naturally we're selfish people so how do we compromise to balance out each other's lives. It is through much sacrifice and a lot less pride that we accomplish this ultimate infinite kinship called unconditional love. Only then can we truly be happy with that person, by giving and showing ourselves fully and freely to them always....

July 1, 2010

Dear Mi Amor,

Last year this time I was falling in love with this beautiful person who was also becoming my best friend. I never imagined we would grow to be the invincible inevitable power of love that we have now but I've always believed that it was possible. Our faith has kept us so strong throughout the doubt, fear and confusion. Today I can proudly say that I am deeply and undeniably in love with a beautiful and intelligent being who next to God is my very best companion in this world. My love for you is pure and timeless.

July 25, 2010

Dear Mi Amor,

Last night was unnecessary to say the least. And it wasn't until I opened my eyes this morning that I realized how much better we are than that. I've accepted that I was at fault and with that I just caused more tension and stress on our relationship. We are different people, Mi Amor, but what couple isn't. Despite our divisions we still work and complement one another undeniably. There's no need for a sermon anyone can see that our connection is inevitable. I just wanted you to know that I'm not dependent on you or on us, I don't need to talk to you every night before I close my eyes but when we do it brings me a little more peace when I sleep. We're both strong and independent people and though we don't need each other you can't deny that what we have brings so much essence, relevance and balance to our complex lives and personalities it's gradually becoming a necessity, a custom.

As hard as I try to be I'm not a perfect friend, lover or partner but I'm willing to learn and accept my flaws and grow to reach my fullest potential because I faithfully believe your love and God's wisdom guides my growth. In so many words, I apologize. You're permanently in my heart thus always on my mind and everything and everyone reminds me of what miracle I have with you. Whether we're apart for a day or a week it's never too soon when we meet again. Again I don't want to be portrayed as that crazed needy significant other because I'm not. The older I get the more aware I am of the fragileness of life. So if we talk at the end of every night we talk, if not God's will I'll live to love you the another day.

July 26, 2010

Divine Imperfection

Our union is a blessing, predestined
A gift no less of divine imperfection
God made no mistake when he ordered our steps
Therefore no matter what happens no fears no regrets
You're the sugar in my tea the pep in my step
The twinkle in my eye, the glow in my smile
You light up my soul make my heart beat wild
Love can be challenging love can be life's essence
But love is always worthy when in God's presence....

November 7, 2010

Unapologetic

Listen with all senses...
It hurts more trying not to care for you
than it does to just love you….
Is it something to be ashamed of to want you to need me,
to be with me here….
Is it a crime that I feel every moment every touch
every look that we share…
My emotions are like a second skin, so these sensitivities
are simply inescapable
Forgive me for any depth that I cause, to me,
this love thing is simply insatiable
It gives you the power to hate and love
with thy exact same energy and passion
What's unfortunate is these words may never reach you
and then there lies the tragic
This outpour, this SOS of unquenched desire
and intimacy is long drawn overdone
My body is drained from this tug of war of emotion,
intoxicated, punch love drunk
Every day I live for you love, and every moment
that I lose of you I feel closer to death. Love, you are my savior,
my confidant, my future and the reason my existence is kept.
No poetry, no quote, no scripture can express the magnitude
you thrust upon my world
You make me smile, cry and laugh all in the same day,
tossing me from a woman to a girl
You make me weak, from the buckling in my knees
to the lump in my throat, to the ache in my chest
to the tremble in my hands…
I'm powerless without you inside of me, an empty soul of cold
feelings and repressed memories….
Love, come back to me if you will, if not no apologies,
no hard feelings…
…and one day we shall try once again, we shall.

January 17, 2011

Dear Mi Amor,

I told myself I wouldn't write you long letters, send you random love songs or thoughtful text messages anymore but I felt like this was necessary. As you know we have about four months left of our undergrad lifestyle and pretty soon life will start moving faster and hitting us harder by the day. With that being said, I asked myself what would happen to our "relationship" over the next four months or even after graduation. A lot of these people we know as friends or boos or joints we won't even talk to anymore after UM. So it put into perspective that soon I will be enlisting in the Air Force and you attending medical school this summer or fall. Chances are we may never see each other again. It saddens me that two people who share the same job school and friends must pretend that they don't have feelings for one another. It just doesn't make sense nor feel right. I know that whatever I say or do doesn't change your decision. You've made that point very clear over the last month. I know that you think this is best for you. But I feel that God isn't done with us quite yet.

You have a beautiful mind, Mi Amor, but sometimes it damages you in decisions your heart should have a say in. Nevertheless you've come a long way in opening up your heart again and practicing carpe diem. I hope that God shows you what He has for you and that you listen to your heart first and your mind and family last because that's where he speaks to you from, your heart. You may not accept or agree with what I'm saying but I just wanted to be honest and free my mind of these what ifs. If you have nothing to say I understand if you share this with others I don't care. I was just tired of pretending, tired of holding everything in.

Most people have encouraged me to be angry, to runaway, to fight my feelings and become numb of my love for you. But I'm not them; I don't love the same so rejecting love is very unnatural to me. I'm content knowing I may never be 100% over you because I put so much of myself in our relationship that a piece of me will always be there waiting. Kind of like the Chu dog movie you told me about, the dog knew his master was gone but he couldn't help but wait until his dying day. So I'm not trying to make this more complicated I just wanted you to know the truth so that I can be free and at peace in my spirit knowing that I gave you and us all that I had and more. I pray that God will clear your mind and continue to open your heart. I will always love you Mi Amor and wish you the best.

February 13, 2011

Our Own Worst Enemy (Valentine's Eve)

Stuck in a society where all the beautifully intellectually socially stable women are—so success driven—that they'd rather settle for society's "happily ever after" riddle than create their own dream world.
See — those Women whose true passions fail to fit into their puzzled life's equation
Because —
according to religion and society there's no room for flawed abnormality--or eccentric tastes of Love —
I mean Women who close their hearts
to eclectic nontraditional palettes
...but open their minds to old-fashioned rulings and schematics.
Women who are self-captivated, enslaved to their family's goal-oriented motivations/leaving behind the essence of life's blessings of falling in, making of and procreating love,
it's amazing—what our fears can break up
and take away from us, women we have to do better
and discontinue with this settling for less nonsense.

March 5, 2011

Perfect Getaway

Miles and miles away from who and where I used to know.
Driving fast, losing gas, leaving past distant memories,
drifting slow
Destination unknown, cathartic outlets bestowed
Luminescent skies, bleak roadsides,
vacant tides of infinite seas frame the journey ahead
Twisted upside down inside out
over Jet covered Chocolate City lady-killers....
Faithful to thee like Common's verse,
reflective of impassioned thrillers
Caught up in life's traffic, 100 miles an hour,
adrenaline full-throttle, nothing realer
Boomerang affectivity, inconsistent as the weather,
indecisive as adolescence, irregular as present cycle.
Butterflies like Michael, chilled spines, pungent white wines
cause delay, arrests mellow thoughts on this deserted highway.

March 8, 2011

Dear Mi Amor,

I'll leave you with this: I know God, I know love and I know my potential. Denying what I feel for you would be denying who He created me to be. My feelings aren't the root of pain or tragedy. I love my femininity. God makes no mistakes. One day you'll wake up and see. No one is perfect therefore no relationship is perfect including our relationship with God. I'm a lot of things but I'm proud to say a coward isn't one of them.

If you choose not to be with me I understand that but I won't accept the reason being fear. I want to make it clear that I am no less in love with God than you are and I know what He has for me or else I wouldn't waste my time pursuing what I deserve. The bible is a tool, a guide open to interpretation and manipulation. One truth may be another man's deceit which is why your relationships, not your religion with God, is only of value in this short life on earth. All in all I pray that you don't allow fear, family or religion to interfere with your happiness in the future. As far as us or what's left, despite how people think I should react it's not in me to hate or desert. I am a woman of my word and I'm always here if you need anything. Call me if you wish.

March 20, 2011

Dear Mi Amor,

Trying this being alone thing, being without your intimacy or friendship is something I must take one day at a time. It's different when you've been in love—it's like a demotion. Now that I know the essence of life and love—now that I've felt the closest to the real thing—how could I go back to mediocre love, to complacent relations. I refuse to settle for anything less, shoot, I rather be by myself. My company isn't that bad—just this room, I have to flee soon and find my life back outside these four walls or I'll find myself resenting my own solace, my own bedroom.

It's challenging because I see and feel you in everything I do. It's as if you haunt my thoughts, my dreams, my spirit; you're inescapable or either I'm non-detachable. I prayed to God that He would release you from my being so that I can move on and stop making a fool of myself because you have obviously let go a long time ago. Most likely dating every person I assumed you were interested in, possibly even shacked up as we speak. Just the thought of another person taking my place; eating the foreign cuisines you used to prepare especially for me; having their hair massaged the way you used to caress mine; drinking out of my favorite mug; just the idea boils my blood, makes my skin crawl and turns my stomach, causing my head to thump and my heart to race from the hurt, the confusion and the rage of being replaced.

However, I refuse to allow myself to continue to be victim to my own emotions. I'm much stronger than the evils of envy and vengeance and deep inside a part of me wishes you happiness and success in all that you pursue—not so much for you but for

God's forgiveness and for my sanity. If it's one thing in my pain and grief that I realized, it's that God brings life to my being—not our relationship. I simply loved you so freely, so vulnerably that I lost sight of what and who is and will always be essential in my life. Though I am not apologetic about how I loved you, there are some things I could have done differently in handling our demise. You made a difficult decision, a decision that not only affected our relationship but our friendship and I only pray it's not too late because life in deed is too short.

March 20, 2011

Effervescent

Girl, you are rich even with nothing, its only love that gets you through...
...not money, not sex, not power—no material possessions will ever outweigh or outdo.

Nothing and no one will ever amount to that inevitable feeling of infinite, ineffable bliss.

Candle lit showers, Sade *Cherish the Day* sways
in between each water fall,
familiar silhouettes shadow the dewy tiles as the infant flame glows a feverish golden orange--lost in the depth of the mellow tunes that linger in the distance,

Girl, you are rich even with nothing, its only love that gets you through croons she, Sade harmonizes the truth to those who wish to see.

Eyes closed breath slowed mind thrown heart grown, tomorrow is yet another lesson, still another blessing,
live, learn, love *effervescent....*

March 22, 2011

Dear Mi Amor,

I fear that I may never love another the way that I loved you. I fear that I may become bitter and sheltered. That life is not a whole life and I wouldn't wish that sort of misery on my worst enemy especially since I have none. I know I was created to love and not to fear—so my life is not my own—it's His. My pain, my suffering, my joy, my passion, my peace is all in his hands so I should never fear, never doubt. I know this is another test, another challenge, another lesson that I must experience in order to become who I need to be—my destiny.

All I ask is a little compassion—an angel to guide me along the way or am I meant to face this alone. An angel with pretty wings, soft eyes and silky, buttery smooth skin matching a luminous smile… ***shaking my head*** damn, why does everything allude to you? It's funny how you never really "hear" a song until you feel where its coming from wholly—spiritually, physically and emotionally.

Am I free, am I really and truly set free because I sometimes still feel captive—attached—held down and back from what I deserve; almost as if I was stripped of my love. My second year anniversary is approaching and I don't necessarily know how to feel about that day anymore. Is the fact that I still acknowledge it a tragedy in itself—who knows who cares? All I ask is for peace—happiness will come, then love will follow. I believe even when I'm not willing to. Yet my faith is indispensable, nondiminishable…amen, Amen.

March 27, 2011

Dear Mi Amor,

The one I first fell in love with died a long time ago; which is why we can't get back to our friendship because truthfully I don't know who you are anymore. It's as if you changed and did a 360 overnight; and I can't put my finger on it but sadly it's like an alien force took over your mind and now you're a completely different person. When I look into your eyes I don't see the person of love but a stranger, a clone who looks, smiles, laughs and functions as my best friend and lover once did; as if the allure has now vanished, faded, gone.

The igniting spark in your eyes that I once surrendered and melted in and shined out deep from your spirit, now barely glimmers, like a dimming fire. Your warmth has disappeared and now you appear cold and rigid, distant to say the least, as you slowly but surely pushed away from me. What will come of us when we leave this place for good? I think, will she care? Will she think more or less of me? Will she be at peace once I'm only a memory?

So many thoughts of you taunt my conscious and spirit and yet it seems as if you feel absolutely nothing. You don't even ask about my life unless I imply that I'm not well, you don't care who I date, where I go, how I live...you're emotionless as far as I can see and feel. Everyone says one day you'll wake up and realize the truth of who we were; but I can't afford to wait for that day. My good mind won't let me. I have to live my life not in accordance to hers. She fails to be involved in my well-being despite the efforts I've made to be in hers. She only reciprocates love and never initiates it. It's this feeling of betrayal, of dishonesty and of deception that I feel from you; as if to be more deadly than an abuser, a liar and a cheater because at least their behavior is traceable. You prompted no warning labels, no hazard signs; and now you show no weakness, no pain, no remorse, only reciprocity. I deserve so much better and trust I'm on my way.

April 14, 2011

Dear Mi Amor,

It's the eve of the day before my "would be" two year anniversary and I just had this emotional, liberating enlightenment that can only be described as an "escalating euphoria." I'm not happy and I'm not angry and I'm not sad, for the first time I'm in the gray. I'm speechless, I'm flabbergasted, I'm in utter awe that

I couldn't see or grasp this before but I'm finally realizing that you, my exe, are an undoubtedly and essentially an "unstable creature," and that I shouldn't allow you, being this unstable creature, to affect who I am or how I choose to love. If anything it just validates my strength and good heart to still love you in the midst of eccentricity. Yet even in this I still wish her no less in your future pursuits…I only pray God have mercy on the next innocent soul who dares to fall in love with you.

April 15, 2011
(What would have been) Our Two-Year Anniversary...

Dear Jai,

Life is too short. No matter how cliché that sounds it is. I don't need to tell you everything that has happened over the past months because you already know. The lack of our communication has led us into "space." I am well aware that at times it is healthy to give space and I respect it as well. I understand that your heart was broken because of my decisions.

Nevertheless, doing things to make you happy is very important. With you the constant turmoil between who I was, what God thought of me, what my loved ones thought of me, I now realize was the result of me being with you. I am not blaming you in any way; please don't see it as that. The turmoil was from me deviating from who God intended me to be; and only after ending my relationship with you, no matter the pain it caused me or even you, I knew it was right. My heart was no longer burdened. I beseech you to try and really understand that.

With that being said, over the past few months I have respected the time away from me that you sought or needed and I still do. However, I feel as though in that you may have lost who "Mi Amor" really is. I noticed that when we talked there was either tension, a lack of flow or even numerous arguments. I made up my mind a long time ago that I wasn't going to argue with you. Although I have listened to you, heard and understood you several times, I fail to believe that you receive anything I now say. So instead I just let you talk, simply listening and holding my tongue. Some things you say about how I am or how I feel are from the truth. Just because I no longer wish to "be" with you does not make me a different person. It does not make me a different person. It does not make me a "monster" tormenting your dreams, feelings, thoughts, etc. I am still the same person. I will always support you and still pray for you every day.

If you no longer wish to be friends after graduation as per your original request, I respect that. But, please don't forget who I am. I was your friend, supporter, laugh buddy, etc. The life we live is not promised and when I die I want you to know that I love you. Whether you receive it is up to you.

If life was perfect we may have someday found that happy medium again…until then take care of yourself please. Love others, truly listen and treat yourself. You deserve it. So in the mean time I'll be here always; to listen, care and support. Please stop the negativity because life is too short.

Love,
Mi Amor

April 21, 2011

Classic (Unforgettable)

I love you I hate you I hate you because I love you/just subliminal words but these expressions equate abstract confessions that even I don't comprehend at times/way beneath the surface-strapped down deep down ready to explode like volcanic eruptions/with so much of everything how do we leave with nothing, once secret lovers, we've now become public enemies as Kanye sings in the background/I love you I love you I hate you, what does it all mean/caught up and in between—lost like a maze, searching for effervescent truth of eternal bliss and infinite passions, as memories stream/complex motions eject abstract devotions—addicted like fiends.

F— society, complicating life and love-mind control is a b— and she breaks hearts and stomps souls with a pearly smile and a smooth complexion, with no remorse she kills affection and any connection to happiness/seeking unattainable fantasies in order to drown in passionless misery so that distant lover memories can fade to black/oppressed by man-made self-proclaimed realities of fear doubt and ignorance, if you want tradition you need to go back to where you came from, this is the new world and love isn't simply white and black/

I told myself this would be one of my classic flows, but deep down I know this s— will only get colder, only grow iller as my love and life goes/your love died about 5 months ago, no burial, no last-goodbyes, just see you whenever, careless here-you gos/ no sorrow no Annie tomorrows, no mourning, no sympathy borrowed/

How love gon' wake up one day and say "I just don't wanna be in love no more"/left love for a D1 ballplayer didn't think love was the superficial type but guess you never know til you know/Drake said you don't see it coming but you damn sure always see it go/airing out all this built-up stress to dry/new sunny blue skies my horizons so high my thoughts are on cloud9 as loves memory slowly dies drifts away, but the emotions stay alive/ baby save the passive lies, keep the polite replies, the phony, mindless behavior is such a waste of time/ the fiction depictions I promise will be your sure demise/ take that fake s--- to the stage, maybe your next will share remorse for your so-called phase/no more sympathy from me, that let's still be best friends game is for the birds that s--- doesn't fly in real life—it's true, actions speak louder than words/ maybe God will have mercy on the next innocent soul that dares to fall for your love's curse/

So gone and so very present, lost in the past but to the future I'm treadding/ pickin up speed, pacing myself, arms swingin, high knees I'm sprintin, passin the finish-line/ hoping for victory I'm clinching a win in this infinite race we call love/I ran a marathon for your heart but you short-sprinted my ass took off like a 100 meter dash and here I am now dead last still catchin my breath from that whiplash we call a breakup ***shaking my head****/ I'm somewhat unforgettable, f— it I made your sensual ideals of romance, your every experience is wrapped around the memory of what was explored/physical emotional plateaus and destinations of no returns/confident this will never be erased, that fire and desire burn, those butterflies in the pit of your stomach, even now you feel em' churn/our past is forever tattooed on your heart as cold as it is, that warmth we created will never blow out, will never chill, its imprinted forever enclosing that ice box you now possess/these experiences are forever manifested in your membrane, as robotic and systematic as you are, some things are essentially inescapable and you can never forget the BEST.

Often times we wish time could fly so that love could die and our memories could RIP, outta sight outta mind...truthfully I'd do it all over again because fear doesn't exist in my heart/if money makes the world go round love is its gasoline, its mechanical parts…anytime someone mentions your name my voice shakes my heart breaks thinking was it what was all at stake/ but God doesn't make mistakes and every lesson is a blessing no matter what takes place.

Nothing and no one will ever amount to that inevitable feeling of infinite dreaming and ineffable meanings. Pure bliss—like a first kiss, my heart shutters from the memory of loves touch, saturated in dewy mists of late nights and early mornings, reminiscing of random moments of candle lit showers pouring/ as Sade's cherish the day sways in between water drops, familiar silhouettes shadow the tiles as the growing flame glows a feverish golden orange—deeply lost in the mellow tunes that linger in the distance—Sade harmonizes "girl you are rich even with nothing...it's only love that gets you through," eyes closed breath slowed, heart grown, as love is mourned.

When we leave this earth, no degree no award no material possessions accompany us, all that's left is our memory of how we made others feel/ I keep that word close to me because karma is a mother and I wouldn't wish the heartache you gave on my worst enemy/see they can trick your mind hurt your body and break ya heart wound your spirit but they can never kill your soul/I'm still in love training and though I'm temporarily injured with heart concussions I'm a comeback full force with a vengeance so sweet, I'm a have to deny recruitment for my team—/Im so high, the clouds are my stepping stones and this poetry is my sacred dome/God forgive me for my neglect, you shoulda been my main, now I'm recovering from disdain, daily riddin this pain of a heartless queen of cold-blooded veins/

On my way to Raheem's believe, India Arie's beautiful to Donnie Hathaway's place where there's no time or space to Luther's house without a home melting away my Ginuwine's lonely daze and drifting away to Maxwell's fortunate, vacationing off to Sade's sweetest taboo--oh love I'm on my way. Liberation neva felt so Beautiful neva looked so Spiritual neva sounded so Invincible neva tasted so Sensual/ Expose your mind to things you neva dreamed, open your eyes to things you neva seen, offer your heart things you neva received/

In real love you never give up on the person you care for unless they show you that they no longer want to be fought for/I never ask for permission, only forgiveness I can't control anyone's actions or reactions but mine, and trust my love is privilege we all have a sole right to our emotions but we can't dwell in misery and pain and most definitely not self-pity. We must believe that past loves are happier without us so that we can be happier without expecting them to be a part of our future. At the end of the day it's their loss and maybe one day they'll figure it out but you can't count or depend on that day because your strength only grows through love not hate or karma or ill-will. Forgive but don't forget/

Some people think love is a fabrication, an illusion, a myth but their ignorance stems from the fact that they've never experienced the feeling; it's a high and liberty beyond any physical emancipation/I pity the nonbelievers and wish them the euphoria that real love can bring. Let's move on, let go and detach. Over with always being the one to give in and swallow pride, put feelings aside--for what? You were my first love but God's will you won't be my last. .

Used to be the air I breathed the dreams I dreamed the essence of my beliefs about true love and everything it means/now your life's estranged, your very being is so so so far away that your very existence is in vain so let's not play the game/The night is young and deep, hearts are full and minds are free/love's in the air, breathing it in without a care/spirits fly high and bliss we share/Physically I've let go but mentally and emotionally I'm struggling, still holding on. It's like my mind and heart are playing catch-up with my reality. My spirit knows what's best but the sweet memories aren't yet far gone.

When a relationship dies do we ever give up the ghost or are we forever haunted/either way I gotta set you free away from me if only to see who I can be without your company/as Hurt no longer turns to anger; and pain no longer turns to danger, close friends then turn to strangers yet though relationships sometimes rewind, the sequel's almost never as good as the very first time. **#Letsleavehereunforgettable.**

June 19, 2011
(The very last note, the last words & the last contact)

Dear Mi Amor,

The fact that I sent you happy birthday should have showed that I have no ill will towards you but you will continue to believe what you want and assume without confronting the source; now if you have an issue with me regardless of whether you "assume" it's going to end in argument come to me. Also let's be clear about something: I don't owe you a damn thing and after what I endured from our relationship ANY courtesy that I give you is sincerely a privilege and gift from God alone. So if you feel disrespected because I choose to express myself from the hardships of our break-up (discreetly might I add) through poetry, Facebook or Twitter statuses then deal with it....Hell, if I decide to write a novel (no pun intended) about my feelings I will damn well please without your consent or approval.

Regardless of what you think, I accepted a long time ago that you don't want to be with me and with God as my witness I don't want you; and with you not involved in my life (by choice) in any way I have the right to express myself how I please. You don't call, text, write, or send word of my well-being so there's no sense in pretending like we're friends and though I forgave you a long time ago I will never forget.

Just because I'm moving on doesn't mean I've healed completely. I mean, you and I both know you never really get over that first love so don't make this harder than it already has been by pissing me off with your fallacious accusations that I'm insincere or inconsiderate about your feelings because you have no empathy for my own. So on that note, unless you have something positive to address or inquire of me or there is some kind of an emergency I'd appreciate it if you didn't contact me. Pray you get EVERYTHING you deserve and more. God Bless.

Sincerely,
~ Jai

P.S. Mi Amor,

After you wrote me that last letter on our anniversary in which you asked me to oblige you and read it in your presence in my college dormitory; after which I cried and you held me and I motioned to kiss you and you withdrew, leaving me, my tears, my pride and my heart's scars for good. Caught up in the moment, there was so much I wanted and needed to say. Yet I couldn't find the words to express the amount of pain, rage, sadness and confusion I motioned through in those months we separated. Though the tears spilled in my softness and lovesickness for you, the negative feelings just would not regurgitate causing me to feel even more ill once you walked out my door. It seemed as though everything I desired to say, that I had been holding in since the night you told me you couldn't be in love with me anymore exploded out of my heart and into my journal, my blackberry and my bible. Letters and poetry; lyrics and songs; quotes and prayers about how, what, and why you really left and how I coped.

Each impassioned note vented every mental, physical, spiritual, emotional and even psychological episode I endured in our break-up. From the Friday evenings I came home from work and instead of studying or going out I watched our favorite romantic-dramas like "The Curious Case of Benjamin Button;" or the afternoon-days I'd take the bus home from our psychology class instead of asking you for a ride because just the thought of being in your car, sitting that close to you churned my stomach; or the nights I cried myself to sleep bellowing out Lenny Williams "Cause I Love You" on repeat, finishing a bottle of *Bartenura* Moscato; or even the weekend mornings I didn't want to wake up, or eat breakfast, or workout, hell, even to go to church; because everything reminded me of you and I lost my passion for life, for love and growth. I was stagnant in my heartache and nothing and no one could heal that broken part of me for a long-time. Even God seemed to have abandoned me at a point. You were so much a part of me that when you left I began to lose myself and in that a piece of my existence; and seeing you every other day around campus, at my job (which I referred you to); in class (because we had the same major and decided it would be fun to take the same courses); and not to mention our mutual circle of friends—I couldn't even rid of you without neglecting them. A wise woman once advised me "never lay where you s—" and my God did I ever learn that with you. Only…I was the one who ended up cleaning up the mess because our "end" was your beginning to a new life, a better life and a life you described as "intended".

In your eyes, while with me, though blissfully in love, you felt as if you were living this double life. On one side you were publicly straight in which your familial, academic and professional ambitions aligned; and on the other side you were privately in love with your best friend who happened to be a woman, in which your relational, intimate and romantic passions came true. Except I wasn't playing a part...it was real and long-term for me. Not a phase, college experience and most definitely not an experiment. Though I was mature and selfless enough to acknowledge and accept the consequences and repercussions of dating an "opposing-team member" I wasn't prepared for that kind of loss. Then again who is ever fully prepared to get their heart broken? It's unnatural to anticipate and foresee an ending to a relationship and that's what ultimately scarred not only our relationship but more importantly our friendship. So in that your transition seemed effortless and I only say "seemed" because who am I to tell you how you felt, no one knows your "go-through" but you and God.

I remember once being so fed up with your nonchalant attitude or public façade when it came to confronting the detriment of our relationship's end that I attempted to put a hole through a wall at a Don Shula Hotel birthday event. Now at the time I was inebriated and of course you weren't there but the fact that I was oblivious to where I was and why I was there scared me because it only divulged how much pain I was holding in from you. Then there were some days, some dark and empty days and isolated cold nights where I would lay in bed, soak in the bath or stare out my bedroom window and just feel nothing. Absolutely nothing. If it wasn't for God, my closest friends and family who were aware of the situation (because of our relational discretion) I don't know if I'd have made it out in the shape I was in. The emotional hole I dug myself into was internal hell and I got to a breaking point where I wanted out of that mental prison and fought for my faith, my freedom and my joy back; and my happiness outside of us and outside of you.

Another memory I will certainly never forget was the Sunday after you wrote me that letter and in hopes to rekindle our friendship I made an effort to attend church service with you. A morning service we frequented when we were together. It was my first service in months and after the break-up and I felt in my heart that it was time to try to be that platonic friend and to get back to God, who was now my best friend. As I sat in that church and sincerely listened to the sermon the pastor preached, I experienced a spiritual experience in which I can only describe as divine. Never in my 21 years of life had I experienced an incontrollable rush of emotion settle in and shake my heart, mind and body; supremely forceful enough to water my eyes and paralyze my thoughts. It took everything in me to not allow those tears to fall out of my heavy lids. I still don't know 'til this day if you knew I was holding back tears in that sanctuary but it doesn't matter; because in that moment I knew I felt God holding me, waking me and rocking me in His arms, in His blood and in His warmth, assuring me that everything was going to be okay; and that no woman, no broken heart and no pain (not even a first love's) was too powerful for Him to ease, to heal or to save.

After that day I made a pact to myself that in reaching my college graduation (and what I knew as the best four years of my life) to start fresh by any means necessary. Re-commit myself to my faith and embark on a spiritual cleanse of all that was old, damaged and wounded so that I could renew my life free of you. All in all, it's been almost a year and I haven't spoke, wrote or heard from you. Every now and then sis' tries to update me on what she's heard concerning your whereabouts and I listen but never say much. The truth is even though we didn't end on the best and/or most peaceful of break-ups, but what break-up does, especially when it's a first love. So Mi Amor, I do still think of you when it rains or when I hear our song on the radio but most of all I still think and hope all is well and that whatever you do you never forget what we shared and how I loved you.
One of my fondest memories of "us" I remember it like it was yesterday; it was some of the last words you ever spoke to me before we broke up…you laid your head on my chest and wrapped your legs over mine and exhaled, "Baby, if you were a man you know I would marry you." 'Til this day it brings me a rush of joy and pain to think about the genuineness and misfortune in that truth because the fateful truth is if I WAS a man we would have never met; which means we would have never grown as close of friends as we came to be; which means we would have never trusted one another enough to fall so deep in love; which signifies how we were undeniably meant to meet, to become friends, to fall in love and even to ultimately end…and that all happened because God intended for me to be a woman who fell in love with another woman who was destined to be a woman who was destined to fall in love with me. Remember God makes no coincidences, no accidents and most definitely no mistakes.

There is sacredness in tears.

They are not the mark of weakness, but of power.

They speak more eloquently than ten thousand tongues.

They are messengers of overwhelming grief

and unspeakable love.

~ Washington Irving

IV.

"HOT & COLD" *(Passion)*

Soundtracks "Silently" - Maxwell |
"Passive" - Agres-her-Wale |
"Thinking About You" - Frank Ocean |

Quote *"Even when I'm weak I still find the strength to love you."*

~ Anonymous

Dear Passion,

(Summer)

As corny as it sounds, it was definitely love at first sight. There was this undeniable physical, mental and emotional attraction that my heart, mind and body could not deny. I never imagined I would fall upon anything close to "the one" on a social network, but there you were as clear as day on my Facebook page. From the first message that fateful summer we clicked, and after that night I would never be the same.

They say the faster you fall the harder it is to get back up and boy did we speed. There was no pause, no break, no limits; we just became enthralled in the pursuit of love. It was almost "too good to be true;" as if God sent you to me to allow me an escape from my past misery with my first love. You filled every void that I had yearned for and missed with Mi Amor and helped me feel alive again; as if to be my second chance.

We would be what they call a summer romance; falling as quickly as we ended. Basically we were the perfect match but because of some personal issues and misfortunes in your life you couldn't deal with yourself nevertheless a relationship, like those cases where it's the ideal relationship but the two people are in opposing spaces in their lives. In essence, you pushed me so far away to the point I began to question if I was indeed the problem. You were the first experience wherein I realized maybe I have an issue with pursuing lovers with issues. I always look back and ask myself when and how I fell in love. A part of me likes to think it was love at first virtual sight, another part of me believes it has something to do with my need to be needed in which you gave and took away from me so effortlessly, so powerfully, on and off for the eight hot and cold weeks that we lasted.

July 7, 2011

Dear Passion,

Waking up next to you right now I reminisce about the day before; watching the sunrise melt in your eyes was the only image I could sustain in my dreams...the inconsistent rhythm of the rain on the windowpane matches the palpitations of my heartbeat as I hold you in closer...listening to your angelic breath, hoping your thoughts are as free and untainted as the natural symphony that's orchestrated from Pandora just feet away from where we lay. Gazing out into the gray skies I envision a place where rain is infinite and sunshine is rare and mystical like red moons and eclipses; a place where imaginations and fantasies are our passports and every destination our paradise, our utopian home.

As the clouds gather closer and your breathing becomes slower, I strip my eyes away from the rain, never fully taking my attention away from you, never. I caress the side of your face sensing you wake and as you grab and lock my hand I kiss each knuckle like it's my last; uncertain of the melody you hum, I jump in and we immediately synchronize, lost in the mellow song...we share a smile inbetween our crooning and lock eyes as the reflection of the rain from the window pane glazes over.

I'm listening and I feel you with everything in my being I feel you...time and time again I assure you you have nothing to fear because there is no one like me and I think you know that... how you feel, smell, and taste all my senses thirst for yours... *Sólo puedo pensar en ti.* And yet I still remind you of the past and I can't control that. Your rebirth, your renewed journey on life and love can only get brighter from here, you just have to have faith...you've come this far but you don't have to fight this battle alone. But what I can do is show you better than I can tell you that the mere fact of your willingness to emotionally and spiritually be here with me now is evidence that you are stronger and more fearless than you give yourself credit...for that I am extremely proud of you and am blessed to witness your effort, your strive and soon your success ... you owe it to yourself to experience what you deserve…*the real thing.*

July 9, 2011

Mystique

To my muse...
This being who I've never known but longed for since forever
Surreal and yet so natural this feeling keeps me in awe
Overwhelmed with joy but lost in uncertainty I wait...
Patience is my only virtue for now I yearn for what I never had
Provoked feelings of invincibility and still I stand vulnerably
Seeking answers to questions I don't wish to know
or hear but only to see...
My muse, so exquisitely enticing in every way,
every form through every source
Nirvana, utopia, and paradise through eyes
that are so infectiously deep, so in tuned with passion
That I drift off to a place where sleep is nonexistent,
the sun is infinite and ecstasy is indispensable...
This being whom I dare to pursue makes a day without love
like a year without rain...
Only time will tell where this estranged desire
will lead and conquer...
Only time will allow me to unravel, digest
and make sense of this mystique.

July 9, 2011

Dear Passion,

Being on the other side of the world you have to wonder if this is as real as it feels so far away. ***exhales, then smirks***...I imagine the places we've never traveled and the moments we've yet to share...your beatific smile, mesmeric eyes and delicate lips...in the week that we've been "engaged," at what point or moment did you "feel some kind of way"...when did the emotions surface and the mystique take root?

For that my poetry, my lyrics, my art has always been a private plea, a cathartic yearning of who or what I desired to be and the individual whose appetite shared that of my own...based on your impression from these last eight days I'm positive you could if self-allowed... ***sighs***

I have to confess if I woke up the next day and never heard from you again I'd still smile and thank heaven for the dream of my dreams...for the time I fantasized and the feelings I visualized...because reality or fantasy you are truly a gift from God Himself. If poetry is what sparked your attention I'll write and cite 'til my fingers bruise, my wrists sore, my throat dries and my mind and heart exhaust... as long as it never leaves and u never bore I'm exalted...cloud9 I want you to be happy, Passion....even if that's not with me...

Your undeniable trust in me restores my confidence in true beauty and real love....you make me feel invincible and vulnerable all at the same time...you inspire me to be a better person, lover and friend...and that to me is what a partner should always aspire, to make their other half better.

July 11-12, 2011 | Miami—10:00 p.m. | Japan—11:00 a.m.|

A Virtual Love Letter (Skype from Miami to Japan)

[7/11/2011 10:45:24 PM] **Passion**: Hey, can we talk…

[7/11/2011 11:25:24 PM] **Jai**: You still there…Amor

[7/11/2011 11:26:11 PM] **Passion**: Yes, Love…

[7/11/2011 11:26:32 PM] **Jai**: Okay. I'm here

[7/12/2011 1:00:31 AM] **Passion**: Call when you're ready

[7/12/2011 1:02:02 AM] **Jai**: Ight…having some computer trouble. Hold on.

[7/12/2011 1:59:05 AM] **Passion**: I think I'm sleepy…Idk

[7/12/2011 3:11:02 AM] **Passion**: I'm going to write to you okay...

[7/12/2011 3:11:34 AM] **Jai**: Si, Amor

[7/12/2011 3:16:58 AM] **Passion**: It's really hard for me to smile right now, but crying isn't really an option when I feel this way. I just want to say thank you for everything. You don't know how much you've done while you're in the midst of doing it. The pain that I feel on the inside will never come out for you to be able to see…ever; but that never means that it isn't there. It's a constant pain, the pain that associates itself with loss; it's a pain that I've never gotten used to and I don't think anyone of us ever gets used to it. Before I left home I could have went to go and see my grandmother but I chose not to. I was afraid of what I might see. I was afraid of what I might feel...and now the weight that's on me is too heavy to bear...***weeps softly***…

[7/12/2011 3:18:51 AM] **Passion**: I hate crying... I hate speaking about certain things, but when I can't write and I can't speak it's a problem and I don't want to end up just breaking down but I feel it's coming. Last year another person in my family died and I lost my self for a long time, a very long time; and to be honest I still haven't found that little part of me yet. So, for another part of me to be missing before I even got the opportunity to collect myself fully… it makes me think of things...

[7/12/2011 3:20:09 AM] **Passion**: … that I don't think I should even think of... I just don't want to be here... it would be so hard to tell something is wrong with me... so hard for someone that's so new in my life to be able to see past everything I show you, but those moments that I just sit and stare at you is when I feel it the most because I just want to cry... I want to just cry, but before I let anything out I pull it all back in.

[7/12/2011 3:20:52 AM] **Passion**: Another thing bothering me is the fact that my best friend... the person who is my strength when I'm weak didn't even sit with me yesterday...

[7/12/2011 3:21:15 AM] **Passion**: …not at all.... She came into the room, asked what was wrong and told me it would be okay then went back to browse on Facebook....

[7/12/2011 3:21:50 AM] **Passion**: I just slept…

[7/12/2011 3:21:56 AM] **Passion**: and then I woke up crying again...

[7/12/2011 3:22:17 AM] **Passion**: I went for a walk on the beach... no shoes... just my music and me... and I cried... I walked and I cried...

[7/12/2011 3:22:23 AM] **Passion**: and I thought of you....

[7/12/2011 3:23:04 AM] **Passion**: Then I stopped walking... I stopped crying... and I turned around and proceeded back to the house...

[7/12/2011 3:23:50 AM] **Passion**: …and all I wanted to do was see you. I just wanted to see you, it hurt so much to know that my best friend didn't care, but it felt so good to know that even though you are where you are that you did….

[7/12/2011 3:24:55 AM] **Passion**: I don't understand everything that's going on in me right now or why the things that are happening around my life right now are happening... and some part of me wants it all to just stop and disappear.

[7/12/2011 3:25:14 AM] **Passion**: But another part of me is so grateful....it's just hard.

[7/12/2011 3:25:57 AM] **Passion**: I know I can't sit in the house and just cry all day but I don't want anyone else to be here with me at this point... and I don't even know you.

[7/12/2011 3:26:14 AM] **Jai**: I want to stop you there…I want for you to let it out because with these things only time will heal. Again, you don't have to carry this weight alone because trust me when I say that every step you take through this recovery, I want to carry you two more.

[7/12/2011 3:26:47 AM] **Jai**: You know my heart and at the end of the day that's good enough.

[7/12/2011 3:27:28 AM] **Jai**: Love, you don't have to be strong all the time...

[7/12/2011 3:28:51 AM] **Jai**: The fact that you still laugh and smile and take time out to reach out to others in the midst of your pain is proof that you can and will get through this.

[7/12/2011 3:30:11 AM] **Jai**: Cry until you have nothing left and then you pray and cry some more...it's the only way that you will find peace so far away from where your heart is.

[7/12/2011 3:31:51 AM] **Jai**: I don't know your best friend but I'm sure that she loves you and just because she doesn't know how to deal with this right now doesn't discount her care for you any less....she may just not know what to say or do right now.

[7/12/2011 3:34:06 AM] **Jai**: You cope the best way you know how...if you want to scream, kick, run, swim or do whatever is necessary; as long as you're safe and not causing harm to yourself or anyone else, do what feels right so that you can get back to a place of some contentment.

[7/12/2011 3:34:38 AM] **Jai**: Bliss will come soon thereafter with time, patience and healing.

[7/12/2011 3:37:27 AM] **Jai**: I'm not going to sit here and lie and say I know how much your heart is taking on right now, but what I do know is your faith...your impenetrable spirit and smile will lift you higher than any tangible source possibly could.

[7/12/2011 3:39:44 AM] **Jai**: I know you are ready to come home and I desire to console and comfort you beyond reason and belief but as of now for whatever reason it's not time for you to return; and when it is you'll be ready to take on any and every emotion, thought or lack thereof...

[7/12/2011 3:42:11 AM] **Passion**: I just want to be home. I'd at least be able to hurt... in peace.

[7/12/2011 3:43:51 AM] **Jai**: I fully understand that...but this is something that's not meant to be understood...you just have to trust that there is a greater reasoning behind where you are, why you're there and who you're around.

[7/12/2011 3:45:42 AM] **Jai**: You deserve to be at peace...but maybe this is a test of your strength to create your own peace in a place you least expected to find and maintain it.

[7/12/2011 3:49:26 AM] **Jai**: I wish I could hold and assure you that everything is going to be ok because I know it doesn't feel the same as words; but you and I both know the power of words, the power of song and the power of love....

[7/12/2011 3:50:46 AM] **Jai**: Have faith, Passion...be blind to what you thought you knew and trust whatever you fear most.

[7/12/2011 3:51:01 AM] **Passion**: I'll be okay...I know I'll be okay...and thank you.

[7/12/2011 3:51:36 AM] **Jai**: I know you will...you're strong.

[7/12/2011 3:53:57 AM] **Jai**: This is one of many battles that you will conquer...just wish I could soak up your heartache and free you of all pain.

[7/12/2011 3:54:25 AM] **Passion**: This is a part of life... and I have to face that alone.

[7/12/2011 3:55:04 AM] **Jai**: This is true...how you face it is what makes you better coming out.

[7/12/2011 3:56:04 AM] **Jai**: Whenever, however you need me, as always I'm here.

[7/12/2011 3:56:11 AM] **Passion**: Thank you Jai.

[7/12/2011 3:57:58 AM] **Jai**: Anytime, Love....

[7/12/2011 3:58:52 AM] **Jai**: ....***soft kiss and hold****.........

[7/12/2011 4:02:59 AM] **Jai**: Let go, deep slow exhale and relax 'til you fall asleep…I gotchu.

July 26, 2011

Night Off

Another life, another time, another fight, another rhyme….
We strive through nights to erase pain,
burn the shame & shed the grime.
Then come morning, life's back to the circus
and we become distant mimes.
Purpose, dreams and goals all trickle down to the C.R.E.A.M…
Pre-exposed schemas of society's expectations deemed.
We argue and dam near throttle over damaged esteems leaked by courage filled bottles...
Served by ambitious, starry-eyed street models...
Some caught up, money praised, material spoiled
and vainly coddled…
In a world where weekends are booked with more funerals than weddings, more prison visits then graduations
and more breakups than reunions…still we've yet to learn,
to grasp that life's too short...
Thoughts of waking up to love every morning,
eating to grace every evening & sleeping to passion every night...
Croon away the worries like Marley, "One love…one heart"…
meh kiss ti earth wit mi spirits and
I hold the moon, the sky real tight, cherishing the minutes of life and love, kisses and hugs and all of thy above that sweet over-flowing with soul, deep soul….

July 26, 2011

Magnetic Faith

Gravitational pulls of hearts.
I remember this beautifully mysterious place of both nothing and everything, in which I faced...
Lost on an isolated road…
Bare, except for the past experiences I held inside
and their stories untold…
Slowly pacing this final destination I process my surroundings,
Assuring that these realities are true…
Fluorescent yellows, calming blues, impassioned reds
all mixed deep inside,
Painting portraits internally…
Each heart palpitation beats stronger and stronger
the closer I get to fate…
If only love knew that I can't help but wait…
With God guiding me through each step,
I push off each stride with an effort
so divine that it's heaven-sent.
smiling on the inside, hoping the consistency of my provisions and charm are enough to keep you close
even if just for this moment...
praying your thoughts and emotions negotiate a deal to keep me around instead of pushing me away...***closed eyes*** I exhale deeply, pulling all doubt, fear and negativity from your subconscious and into mine,
Releasing it into the ocean tides that tickle our feet...reminding of the innocent butterflies that overflow my stomach...
Caressing your waist lowering my head, I lightly brush the back of your neck with my lips...
Wishing deep within for time to work its magic
and be on my side, if just for now...
I point out toward the ocean and as if God Himself were orchestrating nature's every move, the luminescent yellows and burnt oranges of the sun peaks, rising above the cool blue...
and as you admire the beauty of the day break
I admire the love in your eyes...

July 31, 2011

Dear Passion,

I'm finding myself in a familiar place…it's been a long time since I've wrote like this and for something so delicate so minimal and somewhat meaningless, I find myself pissed, disappointed, lost and confused. I'm in between infatuation and "in love"—I guess *I'm falling*. Last night I shared beautiful words with a beautiful soul.

Words, that I wasn't sure if I truly believed once they left my lips. Words, thoughts and emotions I hadn't shared with anyone, not even my first love; and yet somehow, someway I knew they were real…simply because I wanted them to be. I fought to believe in them, even in the midst of my initial doubt.

Therefore their meaning held to remain true. Now I sit here upset, wondering what happened, what's happening and if it's me or you. I know your life is way more complicated, and involved some intense "baggage" then, I presumed; and I also feel that it's something one can never fully prepare for. For all I can do is hold on to my sanity, my peace, my faith and my understanding and continue to pray for you and the best for us.

I trust you love me and I know what will be, will be, for the future isn't for us to see. But right now the devil's trying me desperately and yet I refuse to let him win. I'm better than that and hormonal or not, I refuse to allow my emotions to get the better of me. Too strong to be easily rocked and unsettled, yes I am a sensitive soul but that's never going to break; it will not be my crutch, only my icing on the cake. I wear my emotions on my sleeve and my face; I can't lie, I can't fake or pretend. But we'll see where love and life takes us because just like that I'm over it!

August 2, 2011

Dear Jai,

My quiet times reflect an image so beautiful, it's deafening. I can't taste the flavor of us...but I imagine it to be of mouth watering quality. From invisible hands molesting my soul through a technological manifestation; to lips that touch mine and empty me of all doubt; from portraits of love in the sand; to memories of love splattered on the couches of our kin; to texts that stretch past any emotion or intention from my past and actions that match and then surpass; if I could form the right question I'd ask why me? But I was told never to question miracles.

You've uplifted me so I will stand, lay and fall by you as if you are my own. Truth knows I'd never even fathom you inside me as being too close. You have become my smile...bright on my face even when you witness tears fall. I've turned away from those I once considered to hold you...lose myself in a dream if only for a few hours, every few days.

You arrived when life seemed so low and gave it great posture. I speak of you even when your distance can't hear. As if your heart's weariness still listens, I let my solitude weep for even alone I'm never lonely. Hostility hungers for your comfort. Your eyes always see me as something new...soft and yet irate with appreciation.

These roads are leading me to a place where necessity will never refuse me; and my tears will soak them with the joy of everlasting rainfall. Life, growth and reaching up as my hopes follow. Never doubting the masterpiece I've been selected to cherish. Only thinking of myself in second thoughts; engaged in the most heart melting, mind calming and search for OUR future.

With your hand over my eyes, your lips on my ears and your own spirit in my chest, I hold not a care in this world or the next. I have stumbled upon the galaxy and landed in a cloud of matrimony.

I vow to love you, Jai, through better or worse, thick and thin, present, past, tomorrow and the afterlife. And the day I open my eyes to see you stare into me and tell me you love me, kiss me and tell me you love me. I will sing u a melody so smooth... so "us"... you will blink twice to make sure it's me. I love you. 7hearts for our love... I love you... I love you.

Love,
Passion

August 5, 2011

Dear Passion,

I have mixed emotions right now…it's a melting pot of anger, sadness, relief, anxiety, fear, nausea, frustration, uncertainty, carelessness in junction with sea of insecurity and confusion that I've yet to dive in and identify. One thing that I'm confident of is this sense of loss—of being lost and bewildered. I thought I had found love but in some way or another I keep misplacing it, keep losing you. I know it's only been two days since I've spoken or heard from you but with a deepening connection like ours minutes feel like hours, hours feel like days whenever we're apart. Not to say that's its extended to that can't eat, can't sleep, punch-drunk–love sickness yet but it's pretty damn close. All in all I just want to know if you're okay; if you're safe and breathing and smiling. Life's too short to be out of touch and in this crazy, unpredictable world you can never take things or people for granted. There are a million possibilities as to why I can't reach you, and almost half of those scenarios, I assure you, have run through my mind —of who, what, where, when and how I haven't seen or heard from my sole lover-friend.

I know now that I love you not just because I miss you but because I'm sure life isn't the same without you. You rekindled a desire that was slowly burning out and I'm grateful for your passion, honesty and genuine spirit. Your love has the most captivating soul I've engaged thus far and I thirst for your indulgence like an aging body thirsts for the fountain of youth. You are dear and special to my heart and I've prayed to God for your well-being from Genesis. *So Passion*, come back to me wholly and blissfully. I won't be angry for long because I'm afraid love won't let me wait.

August 6, 2011

Fallen Stars

We rise and fall as stars do….
There's no drug like what I found in you…
The liveliest soul I've ever engaged…so thrown that I thirst for its indulgence like ancestral slaves.
Many occasions I prayed and prayed to God for your well-being, hoping you're safe…
Invested trust and care since Genesis desiring feelings
to reach a divine Revelation…
Thou now I'm faced with doubts & tribulations,
choking from blocked passageways of life's suffocations.
You are…***laughs***…You are a bright red light, burning through soft eyes, blinding operating sight, urging me to Stop…
As the mind firmly whispers *No*….the heart boldly signals take it slow ….while the spirit pushes to Go.
We rise and fall as stars…
Simply because we possess no bounds, few limitations and excessive baggage beyond means to carry.
Traveling through universes, galaxies and worlds far from what we know and who we love
We—resisting immaturity, embracing objectivity and confronting insecurity…all at once.
In search of a love we never knew existed but was always tempted to seek and breathe…only words of beauty and truth could conceive a yearning so strong so overdue and yet…right on time for all to see.

August 6, 2011

Dear Passion,

Okay, so now I'm officially pissed. There are no damn excuses. No justifications and I don't understand how and why I keep giving people like you the benefit of the doubt. Oh maybe you're hurt, maybe you're in jail, maybe you're sick or maybe you just got caught up. Well maybe you're just full of s—. So forget you, forget your whereabouts and forget whatever it is that we're doing. I'm tired, mentally and emotionally exhausted and the most saddening and disappointing part is deep down I know you are so different from the rest; and I know because I realize that, one day I'm going to forgive you and try to make this work again. I'm almost sick to my stomach when I think of the words, feelings and insecurities we shared.

I ask God if this is karma or another life lesson or if I'm really just going insane over the kismet of lovers I pursue. I want so badly to tell her how I really feel but a part of me still doesn't know all the facts and the other part is too proud to care. You love me beyond reason but you don't have the decency and consideration to call me and assure me that you're alright. You know how I worry, you know how sensitive I am to you and your feelings and this is how you act or don't act.

How and why do I get myself wrapped up in these feigned, eradicable relationships with these indecisive, selfish-ass individuals—!@#$%^&*(!!!-- I just want to scream at the top of my lungs; I need to run, cry, yell and ***exhales.*** I promise to God if you call or text me as if nothing is wrong I'm going to go the !@#$ off in the most sincere, mature and unapologetic way possible! I'm too old and past this petty, casual, simple drama. I'm over this bull—. I'll pay the consequences of my vulnerability and altruism. It's time to be a realist over optimist and go on about my life because I've already wasted enough time—you ignore warnings and you find yourself in accidents.

August 9, 2011

Dear Passion,

It's been seven days since I heard from you; and yet your spirit tells me that I will always be the one you miss, the one you love and the one you want. I know this with everything in me and though I know this is true I don't hold on to this truth or allow it to hold me back from love anymore. Because actions speak louder than words and you know I love you. God knows I love you but I have to love myself first and take care of my sanity and my good will. Amen.

August 20, 2011

Inevitable Us... *(Nuestro Amor)*

Mi Amor ......is yours for the taking
As long as promises kept, never to break it...
Your love...I could never shake it
Toss and turn, pull and push...nothing can forsake it
Mon amour...
...is always enough but never truly too much...
Only its Creator knows the depth of our novel trust...
"You" and "I" have passed away...
For since union day, only *we*, *us* and *our* exists.
Matrimony permits...
Me, us to part lips
Request your, our kiss
And unclench these impenetrable fists... of fear n pain.
Mio amore...
Night falls and I dream of us...
Morning rises and I think of us
Skies gray
Rain drops thunder claps lightning strikes and still I feel for us...
This insatiable love...my love our love inevitable us.

August 20, 2011

Imperfect

This world a take you, use you and break you…
Entice you then spite you, spit you out then goodnight you…
Salute you then refute you…
Pass you the controller then simultaneously mute you
Prophets easy to pray "Find ya way young one"…
Loved ones quick to say "keep ya ground young one"…
Friends just like "you got it the second time round son"…
We get lost alone then get found with drones.
Lightning flashes but never strikes the same spot twice
Rains flood emotions into battle mode forcing us to fight
Then twisted thoughts whirlwind and conquer so we seek flight
Crimson Hearts project canvas white surrendering
all feelings and plight…
Reconsidering my personal decisions…
were my past relationships prolonged?
Am I feeling the way I'm feeling solely based off of the tempo
and lyrics of this soulful song
Or am I wrong, simply wrong—point blank…no complication;
these complexities make me weak
And yet encourage me to speak because if not I'll go insane
even though I'm already crazy
I still deserve a handful of sanity…
and though I unclench my fist every time for love
still I drop the ball…then like clockwork all my marbles fall…
scatter fast and far…but desire helps me recollect them
Not in the fashion I planned but the design still comes out beauti-
fully…my architecture is the most intricate…
settle for nothing less…
only the finest power tools used to create this masterpiece
we call passion and yes we master each and every section…
no loose screws, no blunt edges or indiscretions...
I promise I'm so unperfected…hearts infected…
symptoms lead my mind to daily injections of lifelong lessons
of others mess ups and overlooked blessings
Dam sometimes I'm too overwhelmed

when all I really feel is love…
I can't turn it over, take it back or switch it off because it's in me trapped, it is me recapped and will be me like the 8 letters scripted on spouses back.
I'm gone feeling…done thinking…stress way overrated….
pain way outdated….
Instant gratification overweighs me….
Chest so heavy, invisible pressure
got a sistah below surface level….
Breathing unsteady, oxygen losing healthy pace
then I'm resurrected…revived…
Second life blown in my lungs like CPR was my spouse…
In and out, up and down issues we go through,
Perfection is always the goal but imperfection
embodies the soul….

August 21, 2011

Dear Passion,

The reason people end up looking foolish is because they jump to conclusions…my grandfather always told me "those who make assumptions usually end up making asses out of themselves. Well…what happens when that *itch*, that paranoia, that suspicion in the back of your deepest thoughts is right?! I don't know. But what I do know is if that I'd rather ask questions or leave it alone altogether. Because digging for dirt will get you muddy, shitty every time. Trust, it's a sickening feeling and I'd rather not know, or for you to come clean than embarrass myself and bleed out my insecurities. I had a moment of lost touch with reality. Between Drake's melancholy R&B crooning and Wale's satirical f— love rap lyricism I contemplate shutting down and disconnecting from the world—from life altogether. I'm cautious not to mention the word as I feel it's even a sin to fathom the thought nevertheless speak it…and yet I ponder its reality. What power and fear it holds. Last night I rocked myself to sleep. I held my body close to itself and drowned my tears in my pillow until drifted.

This morning I awoke still in shock of what occurred the night before. I wasn't ashamed as much as I was scared. Scared that I was capable of feeling this way once again but this time without the breakup—without the loss I still had the ability to give in to sadness and pain of the heart, thought maybe I was broken, maybe my first love took a part of me that was so precious so pure that this was the product of my heartbreak so long ago. Then I thought first love or Mi Amor didn't deserve the credit of taking away my love or sanity for that matter. Mi Amor doesn't deserve any piece of me anymore especially my heart— only my forgiveness because it's what God instructs. I answer to Him. I fear Him. I cry to Him. Nothing and no one else; I don't want to be tainted. I don't want to be stone-cold. I just want to be loved the way I deserve—the way I give out. I had an episode, a phase of longing, shame, confusion, weakness and heartache. I couldn't explain nor change it, I just felt trapped in this foggy, state of mind. Then I got out—I fought— I knew it wasn't me. God created me too strong to bend over for man or evil or depression or death for that matter. I gained my appetite back, my conscious, my reality. I want dreams, I want goals, I want life! God I am yours; your will, your way. Just show me, give me the strength and I will work hard to honor you and your name forever.

August 22, 2011

Morning Confessions

My soul bleeds out...rushes down,
Leaving feelings of numb and cold
I lost my appetite
But as I regain strength and sight
I hunger and thirst more than ever before
I seek refuge
I seek revelation...
I seek thy ineffable
He came for me one night, ruptured my spirit
and broke my heart

And I almost gave in but then a beautiful voice,
an angel sang to me
She held me close and rocked me slow til my thoughts drifted
and my emotions lifted away
The next day I prayed for guidance, I prayed for mercy,
I prayed to be cleansed
Washed away from my past and armored for my future...
The present is a gift but we throw it away like it's waste.
'I love you' is whirled around like breezes in the air,
carelessly w/o effort
Only death reminds us that we're fragile,
That time is not our own...
That our relationships aren't forever
And that beauty and fortune soon fade
I yearn for thy unreachable...black sand...
golden seas and red sunrises
A purity so rare so delicate,
So unknown that even the wisest man on earth
couldn't begin to perceive it...
Along the way I lost my way
I misplaced my faith
I ran astray
Love drew me back,
Strength repaved my track
And hope showed me a new path...a journey unmatched
Sometimes... losing balance
For love is a part of
Living a balanced life...
*...C'est la vie...carpe diem...Que sera sera...*Amen

August 24, 2011

Jamaica

I miss you Jamaica...
I dreamed of her the night before.
Just as lovely as I remember....
Her scent so familiar and keen...

A potent fragrance of sea salt, coconut and curry seasonings...
Her voice, mellow delicate yet bold.
One could listen to her speak for days upon days upon days.
At nightfall her allure entices even the most stubborn of brethren.
So peaceful and sensual the oceans rock and the winds sway to her natural rhythm as if summoned to obey.
Oh and my God. Her smile... Her golden smile.....brighter than the sunshine, she wakens the birds and the trees with her sunrise, her beaming light, and the purest of lights.
Jamaica, Jamaica so fine...so fine.
No lie...
One day, I'll return to your arms.
Until then I close my eyes and reminisce and fantasize of she…
My beauty...my Jamaica.

August 25, 2011

Dear Passion,

So I wanted to have this conversation with you over the phone but you never called. I hoped that you would but a part of me knew that you wouldn't. While I was waiting I basically wrote down all my thoughts so I wouldn't leave anything out so I'm just going to read it to you because it's a little minute.

First of all and most importantly, I love you and I know you love me. That should always be enough but that's only in a perfect world, which we all too well know doesn't exist. Basically, this past week (specifically since last Wednesday or Thursday) our relationship has felt different. I've confronted you about these feelings recently and all I've received are…. "I understand or I see or no comment at all." Hear me when I say there's nothing wrong with those statements but at the end of the day that gives me no clarity or true response to the concerns that I express. We're not perfect and we're damn sure not normal and I love that about us. But you can't look at me and tell me that we're the exact same couple we were when we left your sister's house that Monday evening.

We can't pretend like we're on the same page or the same

space that we were those two unforgettable days we spent together a week ago. I know you have phone issues. I know you have family affairs. And I know things come up. People get ill. Obligations need to be taken care of. And you can't always be reached. I understand and accept that. I have responsibilities of my own but at the same time I make myself accessible to those who matter.

All in all, I seriously want you to imagine yourself in my shoes. For the last week I've called you once or twice a day just to hear your voice, see how you're doing and each time it rings and goes to voicemail. I text you randomly and maybe you respond maybe you read it. Facebook has been my only outlet and connection to you and though that's better than nothing that's not matrimony.

I've always been the person who always gives the benefit of the doubt. I like to think I'm an optimist and yet realistic in the same. But lately that hasn't sufficed. Because my mind takes me back to how "we" used to be. How seven days ago we communicated. We stayed in touch. You called me if something was bothering you. We talked about the future. Seven days ago we became "exclusive." Made love day in day out. I met your family. Kissed you on the beach; spent time with your friends; spent time at my house; gave you flowers on our anniversary; played darts with your nephew; agreed never to hurt you intentionally and said I love you for eter7nity. So I KNOW what we're capable of and these past seven days haven't been it. Phone troubles happen. Crises happen. Tragedy happens. Responsibility happens. Life happens. But it's the "effort" that matters…the little things.

I've said this time and time again I don't have to be up under you. That's not me. I don't have to know where you are or who you're with. I've never been the needy or jealous type and I never will. I want you to tell me those things because you want me to know them; and because you want me to be a part of your life. I consider you in every venture that I undertake because I want you involved in my life; when I make moves I make sure that you're in my rhythm too.

We're not the same people, *Passion*, but consideration is universal. A part of a relationship, be it friend or lover, is putting yourself in the other persons shoes. Imagine how I feel when I express to you directly and persistently that I want us to see a movie or go out to eat and then you tell me you're out doing just that. Which understand, I'm not saying that's wrong because I don't know the circumstances nor situation because it's not my business, which is why I didn't ask then, and I'm not asking now— because I trust you. But I'm asking you to just imagine. Imagine that you tell me "I want to see you. Call me when you get a chance." And you get a nonchalant response or desolate promises, like o.k. Relationships are about compromise; about sacrifice; doing things selflessly to make the other comfortable and happy. But you know this.

We both don't have cars right now so it's difficult to see each other because often we're on other people's time. This I know. I consider EVERYTHING, *Passion*. I am one of the most reasonable and understanding people you will ever meet because I know firsthand that things just happen and people are human. Trust me, I know you're preoccupied and have obligations sometimes out of your control. Yet I'm a FIRM believer that people make time for who and what they want. And I know if you have some place to go or someone you need to see. Broken phone. No car. You find a way to make it happen.

You are priority, *Passion*, in my world. If you ever need me I will not hesitate to be there. If I have to walk my black ass to county line to see you, to hold you upon your request, so be it. No "sure, maybe, I'll try, I'll see"...yeah sometimes you just don't know. I understand that, but if you end up not making it because of whatever circumstance just have the consideration to let me know; its effort, consideration and communication. Simple little things that we bypass. My bad, Baby. I know I said I'd call, but I didn't forget about u. Bay I have a lot going on this week but I'm a see you as soon as I'm free. Even if you don't get to see me and something else comes up, at least I have the peace of knowing you tried; you considered my time and my feelings in the midst of your own; just small considerate things.

Again we're not the same people but some things are inevitable. I'm not a sideline girlfriend or wife. I'm an engaged player and I want us to win babe. I just need to know that you're on board and that these last seven days aren't an indication of our future. I can only pretend and brush off things for so long until it builds up and makes me bitter resentful. So again, this is me communicating to you for us. However you respond, short or long, with simple understanding or no concrete explanation; how you address what I'm saying at all determines our success from here on out. Like I said many times before; this is me fighting for us…keeping my vows. I'm in it for the long run but it's not fair to me you or us if I pretend like things are how they're supposed to be, and how they used to be seven days ago.

This feeling that I'm slowly being pushed away and that our relationship is being taken for granted, like we're just getting by — it's sickening. I don't ever want to be just content with you. Never want to be just good. We should be growing closer and stronger every day. I won't settle for complacency. We have no excuses. Distance. Technology. Transportation. Those are minor issues compared to what we built in Japan this summer. Let's not move backwards but surge forward. We deserve better. We owe it to ourselves to give this our all and nothing less.

I hear you and I understand, but that's what makes us so unique; that you didn't protect yourself. You didn't hold back. You didn't follow the usual protocol, Passion, for falling in love and being in a new relationship. And that's what new honest love is about. Taking risks. Not denying yourself bliss because of "what may happen." We bypassed the coy expressions and insecure secrecy and overtop impressions; our feelings were so genuine that none of that prolonged "courting" was necessary. If you feel like us making love so early was a mistake then I won't fight you on that. But don't allow that to be a setback for us. I acknowledge that your best friend isn't here and that makes you uneasy, withdrawn and maybe lost; but I'm your partner and though I could NEVER replace your best friend, I'll do my damndest to substitute and be your rock — your comfort zone until she returns home. But what you won't do is fault or blame or beat yourself up about doing what you're created to do. We've already established and made clear that you and I aren't just any old relationship.

You deserve a love that exceeds the bounds and rules and formulas of this universe; therefore, it does seem crazy but doesn't have to be blasphemous or wrong but a beautiful thing. An anomaly of passion, and because of the pace of our affection things are occurring unimaginably fast. It's alright to be scared, Babe. I'm scared as well but I refuse to allow my fear or doubt or confusion to tear me from a good thing. Sour or sweet all I'm asking is to be let in. Rain on me. Shine on me. Thunder Storms or blue skies, I open my heart and mind to all your forecasts and won't complain. As for you saying you over felt and didn't think, love isn't rational nor logical nor sensible for that matter, and in the end when your heart overpowers your mind, just see it as living instead of existing and in the long run, winning every time.

Honestly *Passion*, my love, my heart, if there's one thing these past few days have reminded me it's that love isn't complicated at all. We, our humanity makes it complicated. Our thoughts. Our what-ifs, shouldas, couldas and maybes interrupt the flow. And the bottom line is s— happens. People have good days and bad. Loved ones go away, some come back. Miracles, tragedy, the unexpected occurs. That's life. But it's about your outlook on it all. It takes your faith, your strength and your persistence to make it work—to make the best out of *fukry*; that's what separates living from existing—being better when everything seems worse. So if we want to move forward it's as easy as change. One step at a time; just have to press play and move on with good spirits despite the lows that try to break us.

You said you don't question miracles but we can't take them for granted either. You said you knew my spirit and found yourself in my soul. So let's start living like one soul. I want to continue to be your smile even when I witness tears. Our relationship has so much potential. The possibilities are mind-blowing with what we created and transpired. This thing you and me are special, Passion, and a gift from God so why not show him our grace and celebrate this love every moment we're awake.

We can't deny such a beautiful passion. I pray you continue to stay engaged in that heart melting mind calming search for our future. Never let it go or fade for even a lost second; that's already a lifetime we've wasted away because we never know how much time we really have. So let's not lose anymore…now and forever…7hearts for our love. My love…*mi amor…mon amour…mio amore…mijn liefde watashi no ai…lanmou mwen and upendo wangu….*

August 26, 2011

Press Play

For anyone or "two" facing internal challenges
and questioning life love,
the extra stuff & all of thy above...
If it's one thing these past few days have reminded me it's that love isn't complicated at all.
We, our humanity make it complicated. Our thoughts. Our fears. Our questions...
Our what ifs... shoulda couldas... and maybes disrupt the flow of our happiness.
And the bottom line is s— happens.
People have good days and bad.
Loved ones go away, some come back to us.
Our health diminishes, but in a way it makes us stronger.
Miracles... tragedy... thy unexpected occurs. That's life.
But it's about our outlook on it all...it's how we choose to deal.
How we fight. Words we say. Actions we take.
It's the weight of our faith our strength and our persistence to make it work.
To make the best out of "fukry".
That's what separates the living from the existing.
Being BETTER when everything seems worse.
So if we want to move forward it's as easy as change
One step at a time. One breath at a time...
Just have to press play and move on w/ good spirits
despite the lows that try to break you down and away.
......C'est la vie...carpe diem...Que sera sera.

September 1, 2011

Living Dream (Written to Adele's "Lovesong")

A lover, not a fighter, but I fight for what I love...
No Mercy me have mercy me
Sweet Misery
It be the death of we, of love.
Sleep away our day's decay
And despite dismay we fall to submissive knees touch palms
Close eyes and pray.
Love me far love me so. Love me breathless never let go.
Change like the currents deep and overflowing.
Camouflage like the wild always meek yet bold & knowing.
Lose thyself inside thyself though one could never tell
Hold thy breath and sometimes forget to exhale.
Believe some of what I tell you and most of what I do.
Because half of who I really am I really have no clue.
Finding an identity; finding a truth that's oh so real.
Overshadowed thoughts clouded emotions and hazy rainy will.
Take me away to a time before pain took place and memories
weren't so distant.
Where happiness was simple and love carefree— reminiscent.
Before s— got crazy…Hard to deal
Before Real started to faze me and just got too real…
It's like as soon as the dust falls
and life gets clean and neat again,
You turn around just to find that something else spills
and you get weak again...
Heartbreak takes you back, ruptures your soul and slaps you
across the face...
Then you're back at square one without knowing how you got
there against your will, and you start to shake.
Can't cry but should be willing…playing tug a war
with lost yet necessary feelings.
While some have seen heaven some are still in hell…
Walking dead, cast in shock, overcome by darkness' spell.
Every day we entertain the most subtle yet
beautiful presence of angels …

I was blessed enough to fall in love
with one of those heavenly strangers
Prepared for eternal affection …
destined for impassioned imperfection
Yet heartbreak tried to settle in despite evicted direction
…won't let it pull me back…
Pushing forward, boarding up the past, and tossing it to Goodwill
as we walk before we crawl...
Falling deeper and harder each and every day,
uplifted submitted committed for the long haul…
Still seeking answers to questions
I don't wish to know or hear, only to see…
So gone where we headed there's no return
So high we black out lows, so smoked out it burns.
Years before premature confessions,
distant obsessions and intimate sessions we were had…
Kept beyond self-notice and now we strive for divine relations,
not like before ,but better than we had.
I can feel your pain like Gyptian miles and miles away…banish
the loneliness on your face…
Never forsaken…stirred not shaken…suns set as lips met and
spirits rise to the occasion
Life takes us back while death wakens our realities…
of what should be, the fragility of what we have
And what could be…
As your solitude weeps, our distance encloses
and we regain posture,
in the midst of shallow times…
Continue to Stand….lay… and fall by me...
losing yourself in the living dream that is love…yours and mine.

September 9, 2011

Therapy

Inebriations never felt sooo good,
alternate views never looked as they should
Sinking high, rising low…lost in space,

where time quickly brakes, limits pace and speeds slow
Words make us tender; actions force us to remember…
Captured perfect pictures with broken cameras;
cold and beautiful like distant deep Decembers…
I'm not supposed to miss you…not supposed to want to kiss you
…dismiss you and trick you…
Into loving me just so I can break your heart…
twist it up and break us apart….
Blunt honesty much needed so we get high above captive trees
for the truth suppose to set us free
This caught up lifestyle's much cheated…
t.l.c and therapy much pleaded…
Ego and denial hold us back, smoked out on fantasies
of endangered ambitions of instant millions,
pain-free relationships and eternal youth…
You are my demise, my passion, my weakness,
my power but most of all my truth….
We never let up… even though it's easier to give up…
then to fight back…still we refuse to sell our souls
for faded green and temporary night caps…
Lightning flashes and strikes our flooded emotions into battle
mode…but twisted thoughts conquer and hearts surrender to the
forecast imperfection that is us…that is life.
That is purpose; so not to overdose on this world's tragedy.
Our own vices force minds and hearts into life coaching therapy.

September 19, 2011

Getting Back

How do you just walk out of someone's life like that?
It's cruel and unusual...yet we do it so effortlessly.
I'll never understand that. I'll never want to. I no longer care to.
How one can neglect their own flesh and blood.
Their lovers; Their confidants; There's no honor in cowardice,
only shameful pride.
If we lose our integrity we lose ourselves.

Our truth.
Our will.
Our souls.
Life without conscience or lack thereof is powerless,
emptiness and essentially suicide.
Forgiveness and mercy are slipping through the cracks of virtue
becoming rarities.
Remember ...Crying won't make them come back, saying
"I don't care," doesn't stop you from caring
and holding it all in doesn't make you stronger.
We're never alone as long as God is in our hearts.
Joy is on our mind. & faith continues in our spirit....
C'est la vie...carpe diem...Que sera sera....

Sincerely,
~Jai

P.S Passion,

To be honest ALL the warning signs were there and I simply chose to ignore them and/or were too blind in love to notice. It's funny how we can never sound the alarm until it's too late and we crash or get burned ***laughing.*** That's love and life for that matter. You were always honest with me for the most part about your flaws, your past and present issues and the baggage you carried but in my innocence and "super-saver," self-proclaimed "God's gift" to the damaged, I wanted to be the one who changed that, who rescued you from you from YOU. Despite the consequences or repercussions I believed in your august growth and rise from your conflict, pain and contempt; I saw your potential to love and be loved and I fought like hell for it even if that meant sacrificing my own sound mind. In the midst of my heroism, I failed to realize that in order to save someone they have to want to be saved; they have to allow themselves to be vulnerable; to be unguarded…and you purposely made it so you weren't.

Passion, I don't blame you, I don't blame myself…but I do forgive "us." I have to because honestly, that's the only way I could see the light after our demise. You left me without a word, a hint or even an apology and that kind of rejection in which I never experienced left me in a cold and dark place, reminiscent of the same darkness you chose to reside. It's as if you sucked me into your loveless captivity and then left me to fend for myself. It took some time but with prayer, loved ones and an immense amount of soul-searching and meditation I climbed out of that enraptured black hole.

Nevertheless, as with all my experiences, good or bad, I have no regrets. You made me so much better, Passion, and taught me things I could only learn in misery. Like the song plays, *"we fell in love in a hopeless place,"* and nothing and no one could divert that ominous path—not even my divine kryptonite ***laughing.*** I needed that, I needed you to be who and where I am today; and though it didn't make sense why God would allow someone I loved to be so detrimental to my life, I now know you and us was all a part of a greater plan, a greater destination, a greater purpose and essentially a greater love.

Ever so often I think back, as we all do on past love, and relive the sweeter moments, the euphoric memories…our beatific nostalgia and I wonder where you are, who you love and if you're even half as happy as I once made you…***wink.***

Love comes when manipulation stops; when you think more about the other person than about his or her reactions to you. When you dare to reveal yourself fully. When you dare to be vulnerable.

~ Dr. Joyce Brothers

V.

"UNREQUITED LOVE" *(Karma)*

Soundtracks "Single" - Lil Wayne |
"Doing It Wrong" - Drake |
'Pretty Wings' - Maxwell |

Quote *"If love be timid it is not true."*

~ Spanish Proverb

Dear Karma,

(Winter)

If it's one thing I've obtained from unrequited love it's basically something we all experience—something I believe that we all *have to* experience in order to practice more honest relationships. It's never anyone's intention to be on the shorter hand of the unrequited equation but sometimes it's neither thy intention of the person with the upper hand as well.

With us, even though we weren't together as a couple, I never wanted to hurt you. I never wanted to be that person who broke your heart or who lied or betrayed you. In the beginning though I wasn't sure of where we would go romantically, all I wanted was to make you happy.

The night we met I was visiting a new city in a freezing climate planning on having the time of my life with my extended family. Dallas became a second home to me and I had every intention of taking full advantage of every opportunity that came my way during my long-awaited weekend rendezvous. When my sister introduced us upon entering the club she assured me that we would click as long as we didn't get serious—just for a good time— seeing how you were in a complicated relationship and how I recently came out of one.

Now what I didn't plan on was going home with you that same night, (actually the last night of my vacation) and having you fall in love. That Sunday morning we spent hours among hours in bed talking, laughing, dreaming, loving, and just staring to the point where you had served me breakfast, lunch and dinner. While it was comforting, feeling like I was in a relationship without the hustle and all the perks, it was still so distant from what I was used to that I sort of pulled back emotionally; because the reality that it was only temporary was too evident for me to even indulge in the moment.

That early winter morning as we held one another blushing and smiling, if I don't remember anything else, I remember what you asked me like it was yesterday. You whispered, "so when are you moving to Texas," and at the time though we were slightly inebriated, lustful and vulnerable, I felt the genuine earnestness in your voice even in the midst of your laughter. It scared and softened me in an empathetic way, in that I wanted you to know real love yet I didn't desire to be the one to show it to you. Based on the insightful warnings my sister gave and the prolonged pillow-talking we settled in I knew off bat that you weren't the one for me but as we progressed a part of me hoped those feelings would change. The following week you ended your complicated relationship on your own will.

Less than a month later on what is probably the most redeeming, reflective and divulging time of the year I did thy unthinkable. Wallowing in a West Palm Beach hotel with all my loved ones celebrating my grandfather's 75th birthday on New Year's eve, rejuvenated and anxious off Crown Royal, champagne and my classic homemade "hunch punch" I grabbed my cell phone and texted you the one thing you can never take back, the one expression that takes your breath away whether you wanted to hear it or not, the one proclamation of three words that every lover wants to hear at the stroke of midnight of the last day of the year…*I Love You*….and the sooner they left my brain and slipped off my fingers, pressing send the sooner I wished I had waited.

No mistake, I did care about you, I just missed the idea of having someone around the holidays, someone to say I love you and I miss you and I wish you were here; all I want for Christmas and New Years is you and all that lovey-dovey stuff. You were available, you were current and most of all I was confident that though I was seeing other people, you were the only one who would oblige it and you did.

Months later I became overwhelmed by your consistent adamancy on my relocation to Dallas via your real estate emails to your cheap flight updates and to your career hunting for me. Soon after my tolerance grew away and one day you would call me crying over the phone about how I'm not trying to build a relationship with you which makes sense because you never get who you want and who you get you never want. It was a sadness which was all too familiar except this time the heart-stomping boot was on the other foot and yet as much as I thought I loved you I just couldn't allow myself to be with you knowing I couldn't reciprocate your feelings. I made all the excuses in the book…long-distance was too difficult; my finances won't allow me to visit again for a while; let's wait it out a few months to see where my career goes, etc., etc.… you deserved so much better than that and after rejection after rejection your patience ran thin and you soon realized it too.

As we grew apart, you slowly began distancing yourself from me completely which I understood; but in a way even though it was my fault it still felt like hell because I knew I did to you what promised I'd never do. It got to the point where you firmly requested that I cease from telling you that I love you. It was then that I decided that if I did in fact care about you at all that I would step back and let you be happy with someone who could return the strong feelings that at that point I couldn't engage.

October 16, 2011

I Wonder…

Sometimes I wonder what would happen
if I could flashback in time an...
Flee to the bittersweet memories of past relationships
of "wine'n and dine'n."
I wonder if I would be able to hide the pain.
Or the shame of being hurt once again.
Or even if I'd sincerely try my best to contain
The burning desire of resentment
That crashes hearts and racks my brain.
I wonder if I'd look at them and smile and laugh the same.
Or if the depth of my eyes would change
Revealing from where I came...
Wale say what they lack in trust they make up in lust
So true because ugly truths and beautiful lies
force us to still touch
Even when deep down we know in the morning
volcanic inner voices will bust...
Bleeding reality and defecating on the positivity
that holds on when it's best we let go
Fast forward go...three months recovery later
to the present though
Never thought this day of healing would come,
emotional freedom is such as blessing
Now I walk with a carefree place in my step
and a sucker free smile on my face
Takes me back to the elementary chase
of Disney dreams and mindless behavior days
Damn those were the days...
Before we knew what instant,
intense love from a stranger could be
Before we witnessed butterflies, 1st kisses
and the birds and bees complexities
Now I wonder... if this new feel will last
as I battle re-living the past
I clench on to this weightless living of stress-less realness

eyes bright, heart light thinking only God knows the feeling...

December 29, 2011

Dear Jai,

My heart skips a beat yet I can feel every flutter
My thoughts are never vacant even
when I close my eyes
and they turn into dreams
Anticipation always builds as I patiently wait for a call or text
Upward curves at the corners of my lips
seem to become bigger and bigger
Can one find happiness in such a little time….
Or is there a certain time-frame
I am not sure but I know that my heart
feels like it is forever being hugged
So if everything is good... I wonder why I am so afraid?

Yours truly,
Karma

April 2, 2012

I Must Exist

...I must exist if only to permit un-kissed lusting lips to part,
if only to submit to God's heaven-sent which is and can only be
wo-man, woman effervescent.
How could I not love you when you embody my savior in every
decree...?
Even a blind man could see...such an exquisite creature you
epitomize love…
my beau *mi amor ma cherie*....

April 2, 2012

Nature's Climax

Imperfectly perfect we are in every way imagined to be...
Surrender your fears to the past that prolonged tears too vast
Your touch your smell your sound heightens and awakens my deepened soul
Lo and behold, true love isn't a myth but a reality in which only we could see how it exists
Uncertain of how, when or where
but as soon as we become aware the moment will be sacredly shared
The sky will rain ecstasy; the tides will wave in new beginnings
And the sun will shine on past pain
Then all that will remain is intimacy inflamed, passion untamed and feelings matured yet unchanged...

April 4, 2012

Sapiosexual

Sour acrimony drowns the air,
…overshadows the sweet matrimony
that was once impetuously shared…
Insensible, nonphysical, fictitious amity
conscientiously killing every piece of me,
unhealthy, overwhelming which once was "we" insatiably…
Love, remember when my acumen used to feign you to sin,
make you melt--cringe…
Though now it's intervened our fate's cards
re divinely dealt—fringe…
Accentuated dictions of illustrious fictions
of cognitive explosive,
…intellectual mentions heard and felt.
Rollercoasted curves, contriving impassioned action
to every sensual verb I used to cater to every jerk,
every throb, and every vibration every beckoning gasp
and silent word…

Convos replaced polygamous one-nighter bravos,
adagio, sensually, abysmally *en amor*, still…
Voy a sonar contigo...Connoisseur of all things you, intricately
adept of your every move…simply said I subsist for you.
Dear my greatest aesthetic discovery, most beloved work of art…
and I your loyal advocate, relentless lover
and altruistic confidant.
Sincerely your alleviator, mediator, pursuer and subdue-er when-
ever wherever whatever…See my amorous nature forces me to
consistently perspire compassion and patience for a flame who
complexly desires distasteful sanctions of love-lost wasted…
omitting me forcibly from euphonic sanity simplicity.
Immune to analgesia, we become tainted products
of our societies, sources of selective amnesia
and advocacies of karma-learned sobrieties.
Thy only relief may possibly be detachment, mission Anchorite,
identity re-evaluation, damage control validation highly enforced
and re-applied attraction mission-impossible type operation.
Sapiosexual in every sense, love's spiritual, intellectual scent
still heightens my every sense…at night when my subconscious
flees wild and free I imagine you, unknown and unsure, yet every
night it's you and your nonexistent image my mind still fear-
lessly...breathlessly seeks.

April 4, 2012

Artful Diction

Can barely hold a note but you makes me harmonize
beyond my means
An artist in every sense I bite the brush
and proceed to stroke her *gatita* reminiscent of *Da Vinci*
If I were a virgin for you I'd play pure fiend…
Illustrious chocolate thighs pursuing toppings in between…
Searching insatiably quenching for sweet churned crème
Naturally divine ebony queen I am yours,
To what do I owe the pleasure of your regal presence
upon my chin, your body could prevent worldwide wars...

forbidden fruit your juice the sweetest sin...
If your love was nourishment we'd live forever,
infinite youth without end.

April 5, 2012

Anticipation

Anticipating next night fall...
Reminiscing about love's angelic call...
I got a Love Jones stirring deep in these strong mellow bones
So far—so gone…off of classic love songs, Luther Vandross' house without a home…
Yearning to wash away these pre-conceived tainted notions of love-lost devotions,
Wasted emotions and thy inevitable motions of the heart…
Innocent touching preludes lustful thrusting
Following passionate expressions of fulfilled romantics.
Fantasies no longer dreams, intimately transformed into inescapable realities...
Prolonged intensities as minds over stimulate, our bodies force to emulate each cognitive orgasm
As our lovemaking imitates the sound, taste, touch, sight and smell of nature's deepest soul…
Our spirits console one another hoping for the best
While preparing for a recast of failed relationships past tests.
Yet as Luther trails in the background…
Crooning "are we gonna be say we gonna be"…our feelings sail back…
To a mythical place of clean slates and blank canvases intact where for just the moment love starts over, hearts are free and souls are healed to be…
Newly adorn like never before…purely unguarded, unresistant and unscorned...***wink****

April 21, 2012

Short & Sweet

I told love I'm a keep it short and sweet cause
that's what we tend to need and prefer.
Long-term's overrated because lovers we dated sabotage good things because hearts were jaded, selves hated, trust tainted, deferred.
We should have waited; yet instant gratification entraps spirits so we make careless, anticipated decisions prolonging relations that never should have commenced…memories faded.
We say I love you; I miss you but do we really mean it or is it just the right thing to say at wrong times because it feels good and disables emotions from being depleted.
What's in a word, in a touch, in a text... we go through the motions then lose focus of what truly matters, living in the moment, racing in cycles, ill-prepared for what loop comes next.
No regrets, no coincidences, we all have our boomerang seasons…winter, summer, spring, we fall… tripped off *Earth, Wind and Fire*.
Soulful Reasons then at night we grip sheets weep and ball…
Reminiscing on absent-minded kissing…always a 100 miles a minute and yet somehow our hearts still manage to rewind, pause and chop and screw for beaus who rather keep it withdrawn, short and sweet…
With nothing and no one to lose; the past is just that…nothing more nothing less….

Sincerely,
~Jai

P.S. Karma,

Karma stemmed from our relationship preceding another in which I experienced the same unrequited love that I previously yet unintentionally implicated with you. I firmly believe that Karma is excuse my French never to be f—with; and in love, life, business or pleasure, unintentional or not, if you're bad enough to dish it you better believe it's coming back on you or someone close to you.

We tend to exclaim, well if I could do it all over it, I'd do this differently, well to heck with that…no regrets, no excuses; what will be, will be. And nothing we say or do can change the inevitable. As much as I detest that fact, that I caused you any emotional pain it was something that we couldn't escape; and of course we're human and we can fault alcohol, our past trust issues, bad economy, worst timing but all in all those are simply relational cop-outs and we're both far too intelligent, mature and Type-A-Personality-control-freaks to pull the "blame it on the alcohol" stint.

Not that it carries much weight now, but trust me when I say another part of me, in another world inside my head on the outskirts of my heart, did see a life with you; a new beginning where our inhibitions, past issues and relationship drama dissolved. But the reality was and is we weren't supposed to be together, at least not right now and that inkling inside of me knew that from the first night I wrapped you up and we smiled and looked off into the distance, caught up in our individual thoughts of the future, of the past and present that we then shared.

As the seasons past and now that you've fully forgiven me (hence the friend request on Facebook) I imagine that you found love or at least a more suitable version of it and realized that maybe I really wasn't such an a-hole; just not ready to be in love—again. As much as exe-lovers tend to say this without genuinely meaning it I really do pray you find love; because you're a good person and a great supporter and believe it or not I wholeheartedly want for you what you once wanted from me.

All our lives we search for someone who makes us complete.

We choose partners and change partners.

We dance the song of heartbreak and hope all the while,

wondering if somewhere, somehow,

there is someone searching for us.

~ The Wonder Years

Bonus Chapter

"REALITY-CHECK" *(Pain)*

Soundtracks "Use Somebody" - Kings of Leon |
"Illest Chick Alive" - Wale |
"See World" - J.Cole |

Quote "Behind every beautiful thing, there's some kind of pain."

~ Bob Dylan

Dear Pain,

(Winter)

You came into my life at a time when I truly was satisfied and content for the most part. They say when you get too comfortable and complacent in life, that's when God comes and stirs things up. Well you seemed to be the peak of that unforeseen disturbance and as we became acquainted your story and our future seemed to sink me deeper and deeper into affliction.

It was one of those cooler-warm days that we native South Floridians are accustomed to during the winter seasons when we met. I was working as a canvasser on the beach and you were pretending to be interested in what I had to say. ***laughing*** Highly aware of the nonverbal exchange of attraction that was taking place, I quickly wrapped up my sales pitch and discreetly offered you my business card in which you casually accepted. We both happened to be single yet still dealing with complicated relationships. Karma was trying to get me to settle down and your present relationship didn't possess the head-over-heels chemistry you sought. So it left us in available yet sticky positions. We didn't want to hurt our loved ones yet we knew we deserved "better"—we just felt we owed it to ourselves to find out if we were indeed that "better."

It seemed the more we got to know one another the more I found myself anticipating your texts and phone calls throughout the long work days, and even longer nights. Your company secured me in a way that I could become accustom to. The day you told me you had a three year old son didn't alarm or bother me even though we were the same age. From what I had heard in our frequent conversations you seemed to be an extremely supportive, assertive, nurturing and hands-on parent which attracted me to you that much more. Although I was naturally curious, as to whom or where the child's other parent was, I never inquired hoping and trusting that with time, if we ever became serious, that would be something you would reveal later. Yet as our time and conversations progressed I witnessed and learned things you know exist but hope you never experience firsthand.

The night we talked over the phone and you revealed to me that you were a sex addict — even with my psychology degree and full comprehension of the history, and respecting the study of human sexuality and its diseases/disorders; to be honest, initially, I didn't take you as serious as I should have. It wasn't until later that night that you made your truth evident through masturbating casually, on and off while maintaining our conversation. In my lack of experience in dating an actual sex addict, I did my best to play it cool; as if you pleasuring yourself three to four times a night as a casual sleep routine wasn't alarming and far left from what I was accustomed to in my relationships. The fact that I didn't have to arouse or stimulate the conversation, or even speak at all for you to "get off" convinced me even further of the authenticity of your sexual disorder.

At first, I indulged in the new liberal sexual experience and even heightened the conversations on a few occasions but after a while something inside of me felt a sense of deviance and shame. I knew sex in any form without intimacy, commitment and a certain depth of feelings wasn't who I was or desired to become. If that wasn't guilt enough, your next reveal surely sealed the conscience deal that this feeling inside of me was saying something was wrong.

As time passed, we grew closer and I began to consider you a good friend and confidant. You expressed both your attraction and admiration for me and even joked about a future together. Now what I respected about you was even as an addict you were still somewhat in control of your disorder. In medical studies, these individuals are characterized as *functional addicts*. Most importantly you didn't let it interfere with your parenting and though it was quite clear that it was an issue, it didn't affect your raising your child and for that I was proud of you.

Soon thereafter, you divulged some information that would not only change our relationship but my outlook on life, love and the world. It was a regular night and like many of our conversations this particular one trailed back to sex. With any addiction, there serves a purpose, a reasoning and a past; that night I learned all of thy above and then some. Somewhere in the midst of our sex talk you brought up that you enjoyed very aggressive, almost violent sex. When I inquired how so, you preceded to describe your sexual preference, desire and fondness of being in complete darkness, blind-folded, man-handled, tied-up and choked until shortness of breath all while being penetrated. Speechless, dazed and apprehensive I immediately shut-down. As a naturally visual and perceptive person, I experienced all those things and more in the midst of my vivid imagination and sensitivity. In an effort not to alarm or offend your openness and honesty in sharing this with me, I accepted your desires as sexual fetishes. I showed no signs of dismay or discomfort and we carried on our conversation. The next disclosure you divulged is what opened my eyes to a reality we all tend to put away in order to live without fear.

I'm still unsure as to why you decided to tell me so soon or even at all, but I remember you saying it was something you no longer wished to hide and something you felt certain people deserved to know. It was sort of like most of our abnormal conversations— a random, unexpected *by-the-way* type secret. You began telling me that the reason behind your addiction and the aggressive fetishes stemmed from a violent past; a violent past which involved your domestic abuse, molestation and rape from age nine to 19, which also explained the conception of your three year old son, at which time the abuse ceased.

After you assured me that day by day, mentally, physically and emotionally you were surviving it, through your addiction and routine masturbation; the shrink friend inside of me still wanted you to seek professional help. The lover in me just wanted you to heal, not just for you but for your son and his future. The super-saver in me just wanted to rid you of that terror and introduce you to a present, and a future of pain-free intimacy and kindness and love; but deep down I knew not even I could rescue you from that sort of pain. While I believe there's no suffering God cannot heal, there's just some wounds that even after healing take lifetimes to mend, and even then there's still pieces broken and missing. As much as I cared, I knew I couldn't be the one to walk with you down that path as far as a relationship and a family was concerned. Like I told you then, I would always be there as your friend to guide and support your growth and happiness but at that time that's all I was capable of giving. Weeks passed and we attempted to go out together, but aside from your past I couldn't reciprocate the sexual or relational urges or desires you pursued of me and in turn we gradually yet mutually drifted apart.

January 23, 2012

Pain's Emancipation

I wish to free you of things I knew existed yet never witnessed.
I once knew a girl whose whole world was grim, dark and lonely
And yet her only light of relief was conceived in the same darkness and grief that had caused her torment.
Though on the outside she smiled, her spirit grew wild and her demons brewed with time so she hid the pain deep inside.
I wanted to rescue her soul of the pain and the turmoil
but sexual deviance entrapped her heart,
and I wasn't armored for her freedom.
She lived her life in a way that more than just the little things were needed.
In a sense she was on her own,simply searching for love and

liberty for that pleaded.
Still I was as proud of her perseverance as I was empathetic for her heart damaged.
Because even in the midst of her past she still held her head, survived and with her child managed.
Living proof of the spiritual strength women inherit
she naturally exuded in spite of her abuse, addiction and pain.
So though I couldn't love or protect her the way she deserved
I prayed for someone to one day free her heart & for her purity she'd one day regain.

Sincerely,
~Jai

P.S. Pain,

Til' this day I still have yet to know who your abuser was or is; and wouldn't dare have asked in fear that the person was someone whose still present in your life or of recreating a painful experience or worst the possibility that you yourself weren't aware. As long as theabuse had ceased and didn't put your child in danger I respected your privacy.

I never even received the chance of meeting your son. From your praise and hearing his mature dialect over the phone I presume he's growing to be a very intelligent and charming little man. I also imagine you with someone who offers you the complete package and satisfies your mental, physical and emotional needs. I hope that your finances have elevated, allowing you to develop and possess the independence and liberties living at home didn't grant you.

Most of all, I see you at peace. Blissfully content in wherever you are, whatever you're doing and whoever you're with… I see you smiling, laughing enjoying your family and forgiving and healing from your past. Not allowing that pain to consume or destroy your spirit or goodness any longer; and having a loyal dependence on no one and nothing but God and your impenetrable faith. In the future, even if you fail to remember who I was or how I made you feel, I want you to know that through listening to your story, I felt your pain; I gained an inspiration and strength; and that I never forgot or for one day stopped caring or advocating for your undying emancipation.

Love and respect women. Look to her not only for comfort,

but for strength, inspiration

and the doubling of your intellectual and moral powers.

~ Giuseppe Mazzini

VI.

"LOVHER-FRIEND" *(Fate)*

Soundtracks "Beautiful Surprise" - Tamia |
"I'll Wait" - Anthony Hamilton |
"Whenever Wherever Whatever" - Maxwell |

Quote *"Meeting you was fate, becoming your friend was a choice, but falling in love with you I had no control over."*

~ Anonymous

Dear Fate,

(Spring)

I never saw you coming…but I will never forget you going.

Everyone at some point in their love life have experienced that special someone who has fit imperfectly, perfectly in between those two essential titles of lover versus friend. Now sometimes that individual ends up being a best friend or estranged confidant but then most times they simply become *the one that got away*. Regardless of the outcome of the lover-friend relationship, that person is someone we never really lose or fully let go of, at least not in our hearts. A lover-friend is somewhat of that missing piece that completes the puzzle of what we both want and need for a successful relationship and potential soul mate. Its some-one who you always wondered in the back of your mind what if, what may and what could have been.

Nevertheless, it's crazy yet miraculous how things simply unfold, manifest and fall into place if you will…as if by divine intervention, the things you once owned, the people you once felt and the places you once knew are all replaced or changed in some fashion.

Just a few weeks prior to my 23rd birthday, on one of my favorite days of the year July 7th (favorite number) on what also happened to be the anniversary of when we “officially” met, I walked away from a car accident that probably could have ended my life. With the exception of a swollen lip, jaw and a bruised arm from the airbag deploy, I walked out of my half bent car as healthy as I had walked in it. It was drizzling, as if to add theatrics to the already dramatic situation. You were the first and only person I called that night and you came to my rescue as I hoped you would without question or hesitation. As I talked to the officer you consoled and eased my spirit. Then you drove me to your home, nursed my wounds and tended to every scar and bruise until the pain ceased and I fell asleep in your arms. Despite the trauma I distinctly remember sleeping like a baby; because even though I almost died, even though my car was totaled and my mother and the expenses would kill me—in that moment, in that night, none of that mattered—because I was safe; I was at peace and I was with you.

The next morning as my realization of what just happened began to sink in deeper into my reality so did the downfall of the rain. Everything seemed to get worse after that and when it rains it pours wasn’t just irony but became a domino effect and my misfortune as time progressed. In the next couple of weeks preceding my birthday I would not only lose my car but my job and surprisingly you (in that order).

Not to be overzealous with the puns but it was almost as if God opened the flood gates for my birthday month of July and ordained these promptest, mini-disasters in accordance with my most celebrated time of the year. Like a bad birthday joke ***laughing;*** I couldn’t wrap my head around it for nothing. My spirit knew that for some reason this was all meant to be—in that order—and that it really wasn’t for me to understand or accept, it was God’s plan and I had to suck it up and not only respect but trust his blueprint.

I remember, even in the midst of our downfall or separation

you still tried to comfort and reassure me that maybe it was God's way of telling me to slow down. That taking these things away from me wasn't a punishment but more so a new beginning. At the time being in my feelings and all, which is common when someone you love tells you they desire only to be friends, I listened and agreed but in a way I felt like you were just feeding me some passive, routine B.S (in which I assumed you preached to those before me) in a route to cop out of thy inevitable "I hope we can maintain a civilized, platonic relationship without pressure" or awkwardness that comes with these delicate circumstances of love. Yet now that I've moved past my stubbornness, bitterness and pessimism I realize you were right, that maybe it was for the best…but then again…maybe like with most failed, brief romances, maybe it was just bad timing for us both and that in a another life, under different circumstances, after we've grown into better people that we were meant to be.

You got that thing that someone looks for but can't find.

~ Drake

The following were proclamations of commitment and devotion—a sincere promise of 100 poems for the next 100 days, starting from the first day "we" were pursued **(unfortunately, as you can see we never made it to the 100th).** Nonetheless, I created some of my best work while in our pursuit which told me a lot about how I felt towards you and how my passion plays on my inspiration. *I only pray that in future productions I regain and enhance that spark that only a unique muse like you can bring.*

May 14, 2012

#100 -- *First Encounters*

Dimly lit rooms, Burgundy shades and neo-soul tunes persuade an unintended romantic message...
Initiated direction allured instant affection, summoned to her initiation one couldn't resist for I thirst to be love's imperfect

perfection...
Earnest hands guiding through gentle skin gliding across caramel curves, buttery smooth her deepening valley I browse and cruise.
Ebony Venus, if the more you love the more you learn then your intellect is genius, her heart's knowledge I yearn.
As Sade, Maxwell and Bilal's *Soul Sista* sway throughout, intricate strokes lead to tempting emotions provoked up and down, in and out...
Soft breaths follow mellow sighs which stir warm sensations in distant yet oh so familiar places.
As circular motions increase, pace and then cease to erected notions, it's as if time stops and in that moment I imagine you're mine...so I smile. ***blush***
Admiring each jerk, whisper and subtle sign...
assuring me that my fingers are in the right place
at the right time.
Enwrapped in your glow, your spirit and almond eyes
I envision my hands as omnipresent--
if only to further satisfy feelings long overdue.
Her happiness my present pursuit, obliged to her mind, slave to the way she whines, my thoughts shuffle and my stomach flutters as my hand's consistency melts intimately in her, relieving tension while evaluating her physics...enticed by your "vivid" science, indeed you are art, which explains the dynamics of my inevitable attraction adorn and embarked.
Farewell kisses elicit a sense of trust mentioned, blushing aloud I anticipate the next occasion, the next kiss and the next touch...
if just that much...

May 14, 2012

Dear Jai,

As I read that...
I noticed that I started to breathe deeply not even half way through it...
thoughts of you reciting that to me, made my eyes slightly close, my mind drift and body sway slow…

Reminiscing the way your legs went over me
as I TRIED to calm my urges as you sat before me,
but you did it so properly as though you took
a damn etiquette class...
so with that being said, you're now eligible
to start the next course, cause love the way you attend to me
you most DEFINITELY earned your "you may proceed" pass....
I wanted to turn around...to gesture another initiation,
but didn't want to come off as being too eager or too fast.
...Laying there, I imagined your hands massaging my whole
body, as it plays tip toe up and down my spine,
digging deeper with a upper curve, motioning me to rise...
You pay very close attention to me…
As though I'm all that your SINGLE blinded heart could see...
So, as of right now, you have my trust, and again I say,
consistency is that of a must.
Surprisingly, you have my nature flowing with ease
So if all your wanting is a next occasion, the next kiss
and the next touch then baby MY NEXT initiation
Is for you to do as you please.
For all I would do next time is lay back, as you touch...
if only...THAT...much!

With Love,
Fate

May 14, 2012

#99 -- *Mental Peak*

If these spring showers are what blossoms love's pink flower
then I'll rain dance every evening of every week of every month
of every year 'til we sensually drown in flooded passions of
sensual reactions evoked...
Privileged by your permitted grace I honor the passage like a
keepsake and make my presence known...
You can never be too eager, too fast or too direct
because the moment eyes meet, minds are already erect,...

these feelings growing deep inside aren't driven by sex...
but my arousal plows from erotic intellect...
I rather make love to your cognitive soul before seducing your physical mold...
I'm an artist of all trades and you my motif,
my classic Harlem Renaissance piece,
Acrylic brush strokes our ebony jazz notes and inner cores' peak
Tap dancing inside 'til we sing for more and become weak....

May 15, 2012

#98 -- *Thy Only One...initiated by Maxell's Suite Urban Theme (The Hush-Live)*

Rare and complex us sapiosexuals possess clairvoyance beyond the essence of comprehension...
Awaken her soul like southern Baptist gospel tunes...
Melt her heart like 90s rhythm and blues...
Inebriate her spirit like neo-soul croons...
Ignite her cognition like conscious hip hop lyrics profound
Nourish her emotion like natural meditated sounds
100 poems promised in pure affinity...her holy bliss so innocent it purifies divinity.
Island rooted and bred, would it be too forward to admit I want her intertwined in my history of dreads with every inch that sprouts I hope her present mark brands those new growth strands into a beautiful future ahead spontaneously unplanned.
Wherever whenever whatever desired with these D'angelo "dreamin eyes of mine",
I pray if by God's divine grace we find our Luther's house without a home, Me'shell's "love you down," our Miles' "blue and green" and Badu's "next lifetime."
A life without you is a world without Sade's "sweetest taboo," a timeless space-less place without Donnie Hathaway or like an India Arie's unready for love, a Floetry getting late without the night to come or a Maxwell's on the hushh...without the you're thy only one.

May 16, 2012

#97 -- ***If Onlys****...initiated by Me'Shell's N'degeOcello's Love You Down*

Lips so dangerously sweet she could make poison a delectability.
Her infatuating aura, her erotic vibe, her addictive chi...
Expresses a force so effervescent free that her
amorous captivation could empower the constellation...
Matter of fact... she IS the stars, enticing in every sense flaws
and all...
Baby thy epitome of sensuality she embodies everything natu-
rally created, within her elements I only hope her ocean
aligns with my purpose's design,
and her roots dig deep into my soul's divine...
while her fire fuels impressionable aptitudes
which I graciously exude.
Her air radiates life into my words giving them meaning
beyond earth, wind and fire reason.
Her essence draws me to philosophical questions
Enchants me to prolong temporary afternoon sessions
and lures my curiosity of what may be the seasoned blessing
that is she...
Unpremeditated every evening she engages me
as we indulge in being mentally copulated...
Mind strokes invoke zealous
impassioned notes solely... of effortless what could be,
should be and would be *if onlys....*

May 17, 2012

#96 -- *If I'm Fish You're the Bait*

The way she sees through me with tantalizing eyes
entices my timid innocence to reveal all cards.
Once in her presence it seems I never want to leave, hypnotized,
lost in her heaven, hanging on her every word and gesture...
she triggers my clarity...opens me up for sure.
My Stevie *cherie amour*

How could I not adore, her...
Inviting mind
Magnetic thighs
Inner light which electrifies and outshines.
Nominating her to presidential candidacies of the heart.
This blood-pumping organ in my animate being composed beats unheard once I fell in her contractile rhythmic parts.
As time pass, Interests peak to 8th-wonderous heights,
escalating my mental's aphrodisiac potential,
as emotions become difficult to mask.
That inescapable, metaphysical moan that stirs internally deep awakens when we're close.
I wanna "break you off" in the worst way
like Musiq's Rooted notes.
Total's "kissin' you" plays across my thoughts as I envision a vivid picture of a world witho time...just endless exalted rhymes and illustrious designs of romanticized
Marsha Ambrosius "late nights early mornings"...ouu uhh ouu uhh confides...

May 18, 2012

#95 -- *Say...Can I Have You....*

Say... can I have you...
I mean...really "have" you
Fiending for a love that's relevant
An irresistible affection that's heaven-sent
Weary of a heart that's celibate
Making love to your mind--my body's stimulant
Sensual temperaments contract
youthful butterflies to shiver, quiver and twirl
in whirlwinds of what could be.
If patience is virtue she is the "truth"...
Touch the sky, flying blind, soaring high, breathing life, building lifetimes with you..
Every sense, every breath, every message belongs to her,
she is thy advantage...so real I'd be a fool

to take her worth for granted.
Her being is my destiny; Her team my serendipity
If I'm an explorer Her body's my mystery....
Gliding tongues and lips thick and wet...dipping down tingling spines and sensitive necks...
Behind her ears soft strokes motion near as she trembles
in ecstasy with/in light touches of perspiring heat-firing,
intimacy... running each fingertip
through her dark dampened hair....
As rhythms increase, breathing almost cease...as these circular strokes get deep, the motions attract and eyes roll back until we reach grave peaks and points of no return...all awhile moistened walls clinch fingers...tightening with every thrust cums vocal vowels...Aaaa Eeee Iiiii Oooh Uuu and sometimes Y; and as the warm dew lingers we fall into distant exhausted satisfied comas of lustful dreamers...
Say...can I have you?....

May 19, 2012

#94 -- *The Art of Attraction*

Urges to write, sing, paint and cite
Curves so distant smooth
Lips so toxic cool
As this blank canvas stares back at me and her portrait flashes
through my eyes instinctively...a beautiful woman
deserves a beautiful life.
I grasp the brush and graze the acrylic,
swaying hues never mixed before in stride...
blushing fuchsia pinks
Feverish crimson reds
Bittersweet tangerine oranges
Incandescent golden yellows following
Rich chocolate browns
encompass and overshadow aromatic, chromatic
meditated sounds in the back of my mind...
Suggestive forms and figures shape her image

as the vibrant colors consistently hint unexpected sensations
of impulsive affection and curious temptation...
Her masterpiece speaks to me, whispers melodies
so mellow smooth her artistry could subdue
the most intellectual into drooling lovesick fools.
Strung out on sensuous occasions; citing past interactions
craving next meetings; and numbing encounters
of heavy breathing and euphoric attractions anew.
Patiently waiting,
entertaining
and anticipating
love's next pursuit to forego...
Something like Picasso, similar to DaVinci
and still-life designed *flechazo*...

May 20, 2012

#93 -- *Blessing in Disguise*

Independent Queen, love is all she needs...
But if allowed her heart I wish to endow and free...
When you thirst I desire to be your well
When you're lost I hope to be your path
When you tire imagine I'm your pillow
When you cry, the comfort in your tissue
How do we...
get through the long hours, as time crawls, gradually by us...
indulging in sweet misery we fight not to succumb to its power.
Distant deep summer showers romanced trances
of reminisced kiss and blossomed pink flowers.
Love is some crazy s— isn't it?
Our pasts haunt our present preventing us from marital
relevance...
Prevents us from trusting, moving forward, and investing in...
Prosperous blissful futures…
we so willingly seek yet mis-give in.
And yet something deep within pulls us again again
to strive for renewed tries.

Love, a blessing in disguise...its favor rises and sets,
rains and shines.
Do we lady lovers move too quickly?
Do we self-sabotage our relationships by rushing in love swiftly?
Short-cutting instead of entrusting time,
patience and meaning into futures gently.
Or should the essence of falling in true love be just that...
unpredicted unplanned and rapid;
hard-hitting, impulsive, and unapologetic by any means?
Commitment: the act of pledging
or promising deep involvement...
Forever does exist but it's us who must permit it to persist
and trail...survive, endure, triumph and prevail.
Challenging but possible...rare yet plausible...
We all want the bed of roses but most are reluctant
to make the necessary sacrifices to succeed and lay.
For essentially love is patient, love is simple, love is free...
it's the people who give up who create its complexities.

May 21, 2012

#92 -- *Sweet Thang*

She makes the risk worthwhile
Could turn the deepest frown into an infectious smile.
Her laughter is my sweetest bliss, her moan of ecstasy
my most addictive high...
The captivation in her eyes should be a natural crime...
The sway in her walk would be inspiration for my greatest rhyme
Her sensuality so tempting it could be a sin.
Her brilliance so inspiring it enlightens my being to win.
Before her mind…before her body; I desire that portion of her
that beats, leaks and seeks love.
That can't eat, can't sleep, at the mention of her name
knees get weak, emotions get steep
and spirits untangle and free...
That butta love r.kelly type
That only one for me brian mcknight

That can't leave you alone feinin jodeci.
That musiq love, so beautiful, who knows melody.
That ask yourself, believe raheem
That getting late floetry symmetry
That wish upon a star, blessin from up above,
that no me just "we" team...that soul-stirring,
mind-blurring body-curling,
when the heavens open and the angels sang...once in a lifetime,
Real
sweet
thang...

May 23, 2012

#91 -- *Crescendo*

The musical peak of a gradually rising increase...
Wrapping my head around whether I'm getting hot
or serving cold
Drifting Far or inching close
Floating shallow or diving deep
As emotions become harder to read,
one attempts not to think into it too deep
Feelings come and go like time
but some sensations linger in the soul never leaving
but growing cold...
Many of us bypass the day oblivious to death until
it hits us in the face and only then do we rush
and cease the bluff of anticipation for love...then its too late.
Never one to fancy sexual or material lust...
I rather give and possess what can't be bought...
Your trust
Affectionate touch
and other such hidden treasures that tend to measure
the true longevity of relationships prosperity...and yet…
Awaiting next night fall
Reminiscing about love's sweet call
I got a *love jones* stirring deep in these strong bones.

So far—so gone…off of classic love songs, Vandross' house
without a home…
As I yearn to wash away these pre-conceived,
tainted notions of love-lost devotions,
wasted emotions and thy inevitable motions of the heart.
Innocent touching preludes lustful thrusting
following passionate expressions of fulfilled romantics
Fantasies no longer dreams, intimately transformed
into inescapable realities
Prolonged intensity as minds overstimulate,
our bodies forced to emulate each cognitive orgasm.
As our lovemaking imitates the five senses of nature's soul…
our spirits console one another hoping for the best
while preparing for a recast of failed relationships past.
As Luther trails in the background…*are we gonna be*
say we gonna be…
our feelings sail back…to a mythical place of clean slates
and blank canvases intact
where for just the moment, love starts over,
hearts are free and souls are healed to be…
newly adorned like never before…purely unguarded,
unresistant and unscorned...

May 23, 2012

#90 -- *I See You…(Her Rescue)*

I see your pain, your sacrifice…your blame…
I see your struggle, your defeat, the relief you seek…
I see your sacrifice, your weakness, your fears…
I see your desire, your internal fire, your tears…
I won't assure you perfection but I promise you profoundly,
engaged, soulful affection…
I sense your doubt in love…in happily-ever-after fantasies
I want you to know this isn't a dream
but sweetly anointed reality
A life you always yearned but never conceived
A life with true love, minus the lies, beating, betraying,

cheating and illusive fabrication perceived...
Shattered, damaged and broken down,
Love I desire only to build you back up…
No fiction
No joke
No just playin'
….all bulls--- aside I want you and purely you…
No gimmick, no game, no trade…beau, oblige me if you will…
White flags, bended knees and open hearts in deed…this is real...
I surrender my vulnerability, my humility and all that is dear to me if only to indulge your heart
Because you've been through the thunderstorms and I only want to protect you from natural disaster's harm so allow my umbrella to overshadow you accapella because our melody doesn't need a beat to succeed, flourish and adorn.
If your love is the struggle my love is its fight
If your heart is at war my heart is its triumph
If your spirit is weak my spirit is its energy
If your body is worn my body is its stability
Refusing to allow the pain, fear or doubt of our past
to interfere with this perfect imperfection…
...looking deep within myself, I sense your innocent,
watering connection and if only you let them fall
I promise to kiss every salty tear until you've run out
and fully let go of them all…
and in return I'll let you in deeper than anyone's ever been…
just Let me catch you...
clean your wounds, kiss those tears and fight your fears…
Rescue you from this drowning pool of disbelief…
Trust me and fall deep…deep into this wave of peace
you so solemnly seek.
Allow me to be your heaven-sent rosary….
I know it sounds too good to be true but talk is cheap
and if you value what i speak just imagine how I could
turn these vows into nuptial reality.
Do you think these words are my own…
this intuition is self-grown?
God inspired me to place these words in your charity

that I might save you from disparity...
And secure you a renewed faith of love, loyalty,
commitment and its longevity…
So when I say trust me I mean trust Him, because He
is who I take my orders from, this rhyme is by no means on a
whim…but summoned.
For love can never deter, though may be disguised can never
tie to Lucifer….love is always Christ, love though schemed as
death and evil is only life…only right…
Love never misconstrued…often abused, misused and confused
is the light at the end of the tunnel, the dove in the sky,
the angelic conscience on your right shoulder
in the back of our mind…
LOVE is you
LOVE is me…
she never left, she never deceived…she was just mistaken,
forsaken by those who weren't ready for her beauty... so she
waited 'til the right time to show herself to you, to blissfully
pursue…
For every word I say, every expression I create
divinely instrumented through Him
and you have to understand this to be true for YOU…
And only you…*only you.*

May 24, 2012

#89 -- *When It All Falls Down*

Say love, you know when it all falls down the only way is Up...
On those late nights and early mornings I pray
I'm the food for thought left in ya Ramen cup
Run away with me so we can elope to a place
where spirits are free and love is blind....
Where space is limitless and there's no sense of time.
Where nothing and no one matters except the passions we share
peacefully everlasting witho care.
Distant soulful deep I pray these impassioned words
I'll forever speak and these emotions you'll forever seek....

Reminiscing so effervescent meek about the shape of your eyes
the taste of your skin and the touch of your lips too sweet.
Tensity so thick air so wet its perspiring our every burning desire
causing sensual tensions to grow higher and higher.
Hungering and thirsting for your heavenly being,
your sacred touch...
one imagines that only by the sight and feel
of your pure existence, if just that much...
that I will find the divine nourishment I so willingly seek
so patient I anticipate the rush...

May 25, 2012

#88 -- *Super Power Weakness*

Riding her curves like a tight wave
Invading her currents finding solace in her moistened cave
Outlining her mark with innocent kisses
I listen for climaxing wishes
Her vivacious thighs will surely be my demise...
And this pulsating surprise untamed that I have
growing deep inside my hanes nightly croons,
hums and swoons her name...
Again and again and again
...The temptations so strong my body weakens,
melting at the slightest touch, only a hint of
Seduction with her is enough.
Her smile my kryptonite, if she could read minds she'd be mine.

May 29, 2012

#87 -- *Off Guard*

Guarded, restrained...
and Heavenly Cautioned
Walls built up Heart blocked in,
Emotions hostage...
But I only hope to catch you — "Off guard"

Set off your alarms
Invade your passion's home
Shield you from your fears
Pull you in and tie you down
Hold you close, show you off, take you around...
Hard to read her feelings hidden under her sleeve
And yet her unyielding mystery keeps me further intrigued
I want to know her every secret so I can protect her
from each doubt and taunt.
Wrap her up secure her body.
Protect her spirit console her mind.
Defend her every need and want.
I only desire to catch her — "Off guard"
Catch her when in love she falls
Break down those damaged walls
Initialize her heart's security speed dial and access her system
giving me clearance as her personal 911 rescue call...
Save her from her past
Save her from her disbelief
Save her from self
Warm her cold feet
Eliminate the strain
Relieve her stress
Ease her internal pain
Allow me to catch you — "Off Guard"
Resuscitate your heart
Heal your wounds
Awaken your every part.
Breathe new life into you...

May 30, 2012

#86 -- *Too Deep*

Love says I'm gettin' real deep
But little does she know we're only scraping the surface...
and have yet to reach the peak
If she only knew the feelings that grew

once innocent pursuit became inevitable accrue...
With her my cheeks always ache from rising and blushing...
blood fiercely pumping and rushing because her aura transpires
hidden covets I didn't know could come alive...
these sentiments so effervescent...
If she only knew her decorum impresses my emotions...
Conjures my affection
Stimulates my perception
Caress of her skin
Intensity in her eyes
Embrace of her laughter
Tenderness in her sigh
Love says before the end of the 100 I'll be "lovin," strummin'
hummin *te amo, me encanta*
But little does she know this depth stroke works on both sides
and while my words stride take flight soaring deeper
running faster, moving stronger in her mind...
her heart will soon follow its confines
and surrender to this melodic diction rhythmic wine...
Love...just a matter a time...in due time. ***wink***

May 31, 2012

#85 -- *Serenade*

We all want that…
Diggin the scene
Diggin on you TLC affection
I mean That Mariah Carey Dream Lover Come Rescue me
Take me up Take me down kind of perfection
That Whenever wherever whatever
love forever in a day Maxwell connection
Marvin Gaye Distant Lover,
D'Angelo Heaven Must be Like This complexion

That oooh so sweet 90s Aaliyah "I don't wanna be…" harmony
Jesse Powell's The way you move me the way you soothe me
"You." India Arie's I wanna go to a place where i'm suspended
in ecstasy "Beautiful"

That you mean the world, baby why I love you so much
Monica can't get enough
I mean that 112 Cupid doesn't lie, but you won't know
unless you give it a try
That Case, Couldn't we be happily ever after hereafter
Or that Eric Benet Spend My Life "can I just see you every
morning when I open my eyes" exaltation,
Sade By Your Side "if only you could see into me" admiration,
Me'Shell Sweet love let me please you infatuation
Lauryn Hill I got a Love Jones deep in these strong bones
Sweetest Thing adoration

Serenade you with I want the same old love again
Anita Baker classic feel good
Tamia Officially Missing you, raindrops falling on the rooftop
Frank Ocean's Thinking about You,
cause i've been thinkin bout forever

We all want that…
heart-pounding, flesh-throbbing, mind-hounding,
butterfly stirring, speech-deterring,
Body frozen, fate chosen…incontrollable, consolable,
soul-drunken, natural high urge to love
And be loved in return.

May 31, 2012

#84 -- *I'll Wait*

I'll wait...
I told her I'll wait for her to want her happiness to start
Because simply assuring her I'm "different"
won't provoke her change of heart
Only my actions will re-ignite her passion's spark
She deserves to know she never leaves my thoughts
That feeling that she described as we lay crooning to Kem's
soothing voice, where the music calls your soul to rise
and your body to sigh and your mind to take flight...
I know it too well which is why I couldn't help

but to silently yell yesss love I know exactly what
that kind of music does to us...
Which is why I "feel" you from the pain that lies
behind your eyes
To the regret that confides in your smile...
The reason I look at you the way I do is because I desire
so effortlessly to rid you of your disbelief
and show you a love brand new...
I look at you the way I do because my heart cries
for the struggle you've endured the bulls—you've been thru.
To save you from your emotionally damaged past
that brought you so much heartache and grief
because relations were promised to last.
I look at you because I see you for who you are, where you've
been and where I wish to take you....far away the agony,
the bitterness the suffering...
So don't take my silence or my blush for judgment
or discomfort...take it as a plea to strive to represent
everything you desire me to be...
I express this request in all sincerity...
Whether as a confidant lover or friend I pledge to listen, support
and lend guidance in efforts to mend a broken heart.
Because a life in fear of love is a life in ends...
a life not worth living and I pray you outlive the pain
in undying faith because a woman like you missing
an opportunity to be in love again, in itself is a selfish sin.

May 31, 2012

Dear Jai,

One thing's for sure is that you pay attention...
You pay attention to ME..
Something my past didn't do, that's why I had to let them go!
So that THEY can be FREE...
But somehow I feel as though, I let them take
different pieces of me,
With them, so now I can't possibly be ME,

the ME I KNOW that I can BE!
the ME I hide from and can no longer find nor see.
the ME who struggles with self inflicted pain,
the ME who doesn't even know how it feels to be FREE!
So how can I take what u call a silent plea to strive
to represent everything you desire me to be...?
MY HEART "NOW" is a SUBJECT that's so hard for ME to comprehend so why give it to YOU to mend...
I'm sorry but it's a class...a class that's FULL and can't take any more students...
A class that goes unnoticed so you can't PASS it in hopes of graduating with a diploma or a degree…
So don't put your money aka your heart where your mouth's at with me because my heart's currency comes with a no money back guarantee.
I like you ALOT, but I've been hurt so much, that I feel like
I'm becoming my hated PAST...That when sh— gets real now, I simply FIND an EXCUSE to f— up and flee...
My heart has caught a cold, a cold that can't be simmered
by any tea...
For it runs from anything too warm...
I'm afraid, afraid of the norm…
I'm afraid of love and I'll run from any and every direction
it may now come from…
My heart now, has no more feelings for it has become numb..
I'm just tired of having my heart UNWRAPPED, THEN FULLY OPENED, TAKEN IN, CHEWED UP, SUCKED UPON UNTIL ALL MY FLAVOR IS GONE, then SPIT OUT
like it's some damn 99 cent pack of GUM!
So I've grown accustomed to being lonesome for it's thy only thing my heart seems to know, how to fathom…
It sucks though because I can see that your heart is that of a condom…I'll label yours..Magnum
For it's formed to save, guard and protect MY HEART
from any unwelcomed substance…
Your heart, latches onto MY FEELINGS firmly,
to give me a sense of security...
for I always feel you near you're never a form of distance.

But I feel like I'm getting too comfortable,
like every other damn time...
So just like a condom...this is too much momentum....
and I'm my OWN unwelcomed substance...
so let me do YOU a favor before I BURST
and save YOU from sneaking in...cause BABY I promise you,
you won't be able to handle my labor.
At least for right now, so I'm asking you to wait for me, and no,
I'm not asking you to wait forever,
But let's be clever
And do EACH OTHER a favor
And give one another some space to recover…
I'm asking this of you, because I don't want to be selfish
Cause as of right NOW, the YOU, the I
and the US aren't currently able.
Consider this our very own fable...
I'm here to teach you how NOT to fall for the unstable.
Unstable is what my heart has become...
And ME is what I want to save YOU from...
So take this warning and GO!...GO!...
Why haven't you left yet? Do you not hear me?
Are you hearing impaired?
I'm no good for you...
I'm torn down, weak, broken, marked up, saddened, hurt,
upset...F'ED UP...***tears***
... baby...
I...
Am…
SCARED!!!

~ Fate

May 31, 2012

#83 -- *For Better or For Worse*

Trust me I hear you,
But I prefer to listen to the part of you that doesn't speak
but feels…
The difference between me and you is
I'm not afraid to be hurt again.
I'd rather love 'til the last breath and accept the consequences
in the afterlife.
Love or die trying
I don't care just for you because it's convenient for me...
I care because I genuinely want the best for your life.
Those individuals too damaged to see a good thing
in front of them.
Don't become one of those individuals
that pushes away a good thing because of preconceived notions
of what I "could be or might do."
Life in itself is a gamble.
Everyday we walk out our doors we risk being hurt, being
stressed, being vulnerable to life, love and most of all ourselves.
When it all falls down you are the only thing
blocking your blessings…
For those demons that haunt you are dying
and are only kept alive by your fear.
I don't need you to protect me from you. I know what I want
and I'm willing to experience the ups downs,
sharp turns and bumpy roads to get to the other side of joy.
I don't have all the answers and maps
and directions to perfection but I can promise no dead ends.
No returns. No regrets.
You hold such love
You feel such love
You hear and taste and smell such love
Because you are love
Your every being your every desire encompasses love
So for you to deny yourself of the very thing
that makes you you is an abomination to your existence.

How can I write the way I write
Speak the way I speak
Paint the way I paint
Touch, hold, kiss and look at you the way I do
and not believe in love...
I refuse to be a hypocrite. I refuse to be a coward.
If I don't wake the next day, I'm content knowing
I fought for love.
I aspired to love. I didn't stray, I didn't neglect.
I didn't put off for love.
Because it's what He created us to do and if it wasn't hard
it wouldn't be the quintessential feeling it's purposed to be.
Those pieces which were stripped away from you
are irrelevant now because you are stronger than ever before
with your greatest weakness only being your fear.
I see you in me and only hope that one day you can see
that the major piece that's missing in you is me.

May 31, 2012

#82 -- *My Prayer for Love*

Heal me Lord from inside out. My spirit is sick from pain,
worry and stress.
Create a healthy soul inside my temple.
I've neglected to nourish my spirit, my heart.
Make me whole again.
Wounds ignored for far too long need your healing touch.
I trust you to mend my brokenness. Only you can help me see
the light, your truth.
Help me to understand that I do not understand the vast number
of ways in which you can heal. Your power outnumbers my fear,
my hurt profoundly.
My human eyes can be blind to your acts of mercy and grace
because my stubbornness and ill faith block my vision
which makes me uncertain and confused.
So I ask that you restore my sight and let me feel your touch
and hear your truth.

Because I don't want to fight myself any longer. I'm tired of relying on me alone. I want to be restored and believe in that which is you, that is and will always be love...for now I know I'm ready. I'm open and I'm willing. Amen. Goodnight...

June 1, 2012

#81 -- *Sweet Simplicity*

Drifting on an Isley's memory…smiling on the inside because
there's truly no place I'd rather be,
hoping my provisions and charm
are enough to keep you close to me.
Even if just for this moment...I pray
Your thoughts and emotions negotiate a deal
to keep me around instead of push me away...
closed eyes
so I exhale deeply,
pulling all doubt, fear and negativity
from your subconscious and into mine,
allowing it to stray
Releasing it into the ocean tides
that tickle our feet...reminding me
of the innocent butterflies that overflow in my stomach's peak...
Rubbing your arms I wrap my legs around your own
to keep you warm,
Softly kissing your cheek...
Refusing to allow the pain, fear or doubt of our past to interfere
with this perfection so I promise not to cease...
Looking deep within myself, I sense your watering
and it's the most genuine and alluring image
because I can tell you're almost at peace...
If only you let them fall I promise
to kiss every tear until you've run out and fully let go...
for your healing I seek.
So that you no longer have to cry for your brokenness
for you I invisibly weep.
I listen to your every word your every breath

so I feel you with everything I hope to be ...
Time and time again I assure you you have nothing to fear
because there is no one like me.
Yet I still remind you of the past and I can't control that...
but my actions can reveal my truth and help you see.
The mere fact of your willingness to emotionally and spiritually
be here with me is evidence that you are stronger
and more fearless than you give yourself credit...
For that I am extremely proud of you and am blessed
to witness your efforts...
Your stride and soon your success ...
You owe it to yourself to experience what you deserve…
and nothing less.
The real thing….
When I make moves I hope that one day
you're in those rhythms too.
My desire isn't to go too hard or fast
but sometimes fate over compasses time.
We bypassed the coy expressions, the insecure secrecy
and over the top impressions because
our feelings were so genuine
that none of that prolonged "courting" were necessary.
You deserve a love that exceeds the bounds, rules
and formulas of this universe.
An anomaly of passion, sour or sweet — all I'm asking
is to be let in.
Rain on me. Shine on me.
Thunder Storms or Blue skies
I open my heart and mind to all your forecasts
and won't complain.
Real Love isn't rational, logical nor sensible for that matter and
In the end when your heart overpowers your mind
just see it as "living" instead of existing
and in the long run, winning
even if we lose now and then.
If there's one thing these experiences have reminded me
it's that love isn't complicated at all.
We, our humanity makes it too hard.

Our thoughts…. Our "what ifs, shoulda-couldas and maybes"
interrupt the flow.
And the bottom line is s— happens.
Miracles, tragedy tho unexpected, they come and go.
But it's about our outlook on it all that keeps us afloat.
Your faith your strength and your persistence
are what makes it work.
To make the best out of *fukry*
That's what separates living from existing.
Being better when everything seems worse.
So if you want to move forward it's as easy as change.
One step at a time….
Just allow your finger to press play and move on
with good spirits,
despite the lows that try to break it.
Yeah, sometimes condoms bust especially
with the force and power a magnum brings...
but trust I can withstand your painstaking labor
because if this sacred protection yields to our divine connection
then just imagine the passionate blessing
that we'll birth in its means.

June 3, 2012

#80 -- *Vindications*

Her portrait lingers in my fingers so I stroke her figure
if only to remember.
Through spiritual lens I see her as the perfect picture.
Flaws and all I want it all.
My caramel, chocolate high the more I consume
the more I got to have.
Her smile her eyes are imprinted in my soul
til thy end of time. Sunday morning blessing
I imagine the potential her love rests in.
In a world of dark pain and ill faith she illuminates my skies,
rises the day into the night, brings meaning to believing
and makes it worth the fight.

As she ponders about my mind, my intention,
my existence to her willing...I assure that
My quiet serves as a silent prayer giving grace
to the moments that were shared.
As an analyst I can't help but examine everything thought,
felt, said and what was not...
I bask in taking advantage of every morsel, portion
and sense of my emotions, so I dig deep,
too deep in my psyche and think of every instance,
every word, every laugh, every verb…
Each interaction heightens my attraction
actively stimulating my next intimate reaction toward us.
The next touch, next rub, the next seduction
cultivates my cognition into such a rush
that my mind can't help but wonder…
What, where, why and how I was chosen to wait for her love...
but I feel it stems from above.
Because it never escapes my captivation.
Trails in my infatuation.
Pulls my spirit's mediation
and calls my soul to uproar in vindication…to love.

June 4, 2012

#79 -- *The Little Things*

If desiring love is wrong I don't want to be right
If we meet in the stars then baby I can't wait until the night
We live and give, take and make, grow to know...
and sometimes get built up just to break and blow
So Hurt, fight, struggle no more...relief, freedom, bliss waits on the other side of the door....
Everyday we pray for God's grace to save us from ourselves and forgive past sins in his name sake
Yea though I walk through the valley of the shadow of death I shall fear no evil...
because as long as love's in my heart
faith stays on my mind

and compassion's in my soul...you can withstand life's upheaval
Close your eyes and breathe slow and deep
Envision yourself rising above lifeless weight that drowns your hope, enforces you to sink
Hold my hand as we glide to distant lands where our spirits fly and emotions have no disguise nor meet their demise.
Just simplicity at its best....
No stress
No fret
No mess to detect.....just divine progress, success
and for better or for worse acquiesce...
Less than perfect yes, because normal's outdated and oblique,
fame and fortune—an overrated mystique...for its L.O.V.E,
though we won't admit, we all so desperately seek...
the bliss in a kiss
the grace in an embrace
the chance found in a gripped hand
the smile that glistens in promising eyes
the rain that washes away our pain and instills our peace
the wind that whirls away our grief
the trees that root our dreams
the oceans that overflow and balance our esteem
...the natural presence of spiritual luminescence
in all its glory and flourished essence...
it's the little things we deem
the little things that we sometimes fail
to sincerely see and retrieve
the little things that matter and yet it seems
it's the little things we overlook yet they hold virtuous power
in a world filled with false glitz and gleam.

June 5, 2012

#78 -- *Prayed Up Freestyle*

Prayed up Raised up,
Dazed up, in a zone
Languish the anguish

Blazed up super gone
Weighed up extra strong
Phased up freshly grown
Initiated Anticipated
underrated yet heaven known
Armed, prepped,
Ready for whatever
Adaptive, strapped in
unpredicted weather
So We hustle and Aim together
strive and regain for the better
My purpose didactic
My dialect emphatic
My love so impassioned
I Declare my sincerity
is no guile just good habit.
My lover and other half thy baddest
My charm and intellect genuine,
No tactics
My skill is so menacing its damn near attractive.
Though my heart's wild
my soul's mild
my mind gone
My feelin's strong
So I can't go wrong
God's child so my soul's home grown...

June 6, 2012

#77 -- Te Extrano

Te extrano like I miss a good thing
Cool Ocean tides
Hot bubble baths
Road trip sights
Summer barbeque laughs

Te extrano like I miss a distant lover
An Intimate massage

A private retreat
Puppy love facades
Long walks on the beach

Te extrano like I miss my childhood
Homemade meals
Family vacations
Adolescent frills
First time sensations

Te extrano and every piece that is you
That seductive smile
Those dreamy eyes that drive me wild
That passionate expression, those succulent lips
That tempting tongue and alluring hips
I miss her natural aggression
Her arousal my obsession
imperfect perfection my frequent flyer miles in automatic registry for her location
Her sensual mental playlist my favorite selection so it stays in constant rotation.
If my romance was a novel series she'd be scripted in each dedication.
Something similar to *flechazo*
so in case I never see tomorrow love you knew for sure
te extrano...

June 7, 2012

#76 -- *May 7th*

Four weeks ago what began as an innocent crush...
Romanced overtime into a cultivated trust....
Far exceeding fatal attraction, sensuous attachment or casual lust...
Tip toeing in realms of serendipity flowing, karmic knowing and divine decree sowing much.
Four weeks ago I stumbled upon a precious jewel...
An angelic gift which shattered all once ill-faithed myths that *flechazo* didn't exist...

Four weeks ago I didn't know
Who Love was
Or where this would go
Four weeks ago I wasn't sure
If these feelings were pure
Or how I could elect a cure
for this emotion's allure....
In hopes to further endure and secure Love's assure and demure appeal and reason....
Four weeks today I give grace and pray that this feeling lasts more than just a season.
Four weeks today I give thanks to God for blessings in love that again can be believed in.

June 8, 2012

#75 -- *Pleasance*

Pleasance (n): *a fundamental feeling that is hard to define but that people desire to experience.*

"On a regular" deep vernacular initially enticed
and attracted her...
Impassioned verbs penetrated predicated mental orgasms
unheard like a heart embezzler.
Attention and sweetness weathered her storms away...
Enlightened her rain...shined rays on her cold feet
and battered cloudy days...
It's like we anticipate the best but prepare for the worst
yet in the mix get lost and neglect the fact that we're blessed
beyond what we thirst.
With love I know this much to be true...
It's the only thing that's real with such fiction who knew...
Simply going on a carpe diem whim and chance;
opening weary eyes to *que sera sera* romance...
Never assume never infer...for blushing emotions
can always deter...
I can taste the pain, love and desire on moistened lips...
spiced just right like a fiery curry taste.

The flavored temptation bites and spites my tongue, yet I crave for more because my appetite for her affection yearns the chase. Bittersweet like chamomile honey lemon tea...I only urge and seek to quench her parched thirst, fiendish hunger and vacant anima decree.
Her essence the most precious pleasance ...every day with her is like Christmas, spring and New Year's Eve enwrapped in heaven ....my pleasance....***wink***

June 10, 2012

#74 -- *Linger*

Hoping to linger emotively in thoughts, melodies and dreams...
As India's ready for love bellows in the distance one hopes to linger in that our presence is forever deemed.
Linger like acoustic soul,
like island flavors bold
Linger like secrets which unfold...
Like love stories untold...
Hopes to linger in her pillows between her sheets
Hopes to linger in every touch we feel every sound we hear every image we see.
Linger in her smile her laughter her stubborn pride...
I pray we linger in the back of love's mind...
Never to hide
never to lie
But Only to confide and in the hopes to last
and surpass devil's doubt and evil's fearful passing tides.
We linger like a bittersweet taste dipped in faith.
Like an inevitable routine effortlessly made.
I hope to linger never reaching apathy.
Linger like blissful memory
Altruistic empathy
and distant fond reality.
Linger like imprints on the soul flourishing.
Linger like chi town rainy nights *love jones* urgency.

June 10, 2012

#73 -- *Waiting to Exhale*

Sunday evening blues without the grieving...
Whitney Houston preacher's wife tunes harmonizing
"I believe in..."
Lights low, sweet incense burning...
Souls high,
Kindred spirits yearning
To live and know true meanings
Of the simplicity of life freedoms
And the complexity of love reasons
Thoughts tip toe in the back of my
... Mind of black stride and the honor and consequence of pride.
Humble beginnings, holding true from how far we've come.
Waiting to exhale dreaming
Chasing a good thing fiending
Drifting off in hopes of lifting locks in tells of my deepest fears, flaws and fails.
With every new tomorrow
I bite the bullets of past sorrow
Deep breath...whispering no regrets...then repeat ****Exhale****

June 11, 2012

#72 -- *New Life*

Sometimes we have to die a little inside to experience new life...
Shed old skin of the past and release demons that rest deep within, so fear you can defy...
New life promotes new beginnings, new experiences and instant delivery from self-misery...
A rebirth of mind body and soul....a spiritual release of the old and its afflictive antiques we once stored
New life brings an ineffable healing that can't be bought only seeked...
...open the door to the captive closet of lost feelings you once bore...

only love can inspire new life...its intimacy transpires new direction and arouses cognitive erections of happily ever after type perfection...
Breathe new life into your present and imagine a life where you're actually ready...
it's almost breath-taking if you let it...***(((*exhales*)))***...
a life where canvases are blank...slates are clean and hearts are open, free and virginal like the first time...
Untainted, liberated, invigorated...new life is thy essence of growth...
growth in the inevitable...growth from the penetrable...growth to the intelligible mind space to promote
what feels right...what deserves our plight...how to know when to take flight and when to fight...
see new life strives to fulfill "the non-replenishable" and sincerely instill...
Therefore its success is only possible through good faith and strong will...
They say All is fair in love...yet while fallin comes easy, it's the "stayin" that trips us up.
New life brings great anticipation but a wise man once said never be too anxious...
for God's time is sanctioned and when the right time comes you'll face it and have no doubt or question that new life has begun...and with it comes new pure hidden treasures and blessings...

June 12, 2012

#71 -- *Poetic Plight*

I tend to write 'til I feel no more... inflamed words simmer through fiery lips only quenched by a moistened literary fix...in which I can't help but recite for I fiend for more...
Poetic plight that I can't resist for it entices my very core...
A Renaissance addict for this artistic habit—these lyrics, motifs and ballads I was destined to adore...
Art, my beau...My lover...*Ma cherie amour...*

This expressive art that seeps through effervescent parts
'til it pours...
Stricken my cognition with a feverish heat
which ignites my sensitive condition so severe
that no ancient herb can treat its disease so my spirit leaks...
these rhythmic dictions…
Which stir and burn intellectual peaks...
This art that attracted my young heart to prolifically push start
and soulfully embark on this aesthetic, prophetic journey
of liberal culture and intuitive emotion...
Poetic justice; she will always have my devotion
Been with me from the start...
I will infinitely be intertwined in her motion...
This art I fell in love with since the beginning
she's had my heart my soul.
Quintessential language...this art my life story told....

June 13, 2012

#70 -- *Never Wanna Leave*

I never wanna leave...
So I tend to stay in no dismay, way past scheduled time...
I never wanna leave
Because when she's close to me I can feel her heartbeat in sync with mine.
I never wanna leave
Because the angelic air she breathes while under me
is so peacefully sweet it calls my soul to sing.
I never wanna leave
For she asks me not to go away
I never wanna leave
Because her kiss permits me to be free insisting that I never stray
I never wanna leave
So I tend to tempt and tease she until love relaxes her chi (chee)
because of anticipating uncertainty of our next encounter of pure intimacy.
I never wanna leave

Because a part of me wonders if she'll
remember me the next day.
I never wanna leave
So when I stay I assure I show grace and every second
of every minute I make efforts to embrace
and caress her face
as indulgent as it seems.
I never wanna leave
...because undeniably only Heaven knows
what tomorrow brings...

June 14, 2012

#69 -- *Mona Lisa*

The deeper I get into your portrait the more attracted I become...
Your features have a flawless rhythm, a fluid motion that entices
so persuasive I succumb...
The intensity in your eyes so boldly entrancing...
Your lips so fully defined and sensually romancing...
Dark hair so illustrious silky smooth my ink
leaks her beautiful truth...
Her figure my mind subdues so when I outline her curves
my hands begin to jerk, swerve and cruise...
Into an intrinsic stroke so naturally flowing...
that my paint brush provokes her hues so vividly cool
it ensues a vibe so freshly new that her canvas dances on my
finger tips shading eyes, lips, cheeks
and soft hair I so sincerely miss...
As an artist I crave her masterpiece for it inspires me
so faithfully that I create to please her...
Hopeful that if I persistently strive to be reminiscent
of Da Vinci in my artistry she'll one day be my Mona Lisa...

June 15, 2012

#68 -- *Matrimony*

The union of two in life is what we adamantly,
emphatically pursue...
A consistent affection, a persistent detection
of what it means to love, be loved
and the maintenance of feelings construed.
We survive off of our connections to others
who favor our attractions so it's natural
to desire the natural—matrimony...
The selfless commitment of fidelity
The relentless perseverance
of loyalty
The undeniable reliable companionship of a best friend.
The consistent, persistence to fall in love over and over again.
The empowering faith it takes to fight for a relationship
versus giving in.
The romanced passion that re-ignites love-lost fashions
which endlessly inspires us to win...
Matrimony although not always what its seems
in the midst of the symbolic rings
The wedding celebration gleams
and enthused sensationalism that marriage brings...
For the ideals, the art, the vows of Matrimony
signifies a far deeper, spiritual and infinite means...matrimony,
a bittersweet, quintessential, beautiful thing.

June 16, 2012

#67 -- *Last Kiss*

I want you to kiss me like you'll never see me again...
Touch me like my very next breath depends on the caress of your
delicate hands.
That crazy lazy love, I fight not to indulge in her impenetrable
hold, her irresistible hugs.
Every time I leave it's that last kiss that stirs something ineffable

deep inside me, rushing wild.
That last kiss, so anticipated yet secretly hated because we know it's the last time for a while.
I only pray that a "while" never turns into what seems like forever Her side of the bed is my constant solace before my exit, my purposely prolonged closing endeavor.
That last kiss I always miss
That last kiss the hardest to resist
That last kiss my coveted bliss
That last kiss the most intimate
The most physical
The most intricate
That last kiss I always struggle with...
Because after we release, it replays in my head time after time...
until lips are met again and the moments
no longer linger in my mind.

June 20, 2012

#66 -- *Sweet Disenchantment*

We all fear and thus stray from the people places and things, which adhere to that which isn't clear...
That is the Dark, the strange
The dangerous, the difficult
And most of all the deep...
Air thick and heavy, mind soaring blind and deadly,
heart hungers steady, grumbles for the passion
it so tempestuously seeks...
We all begin as loveless strangers roaming around
life's serendipity aimless until in *Fate* we finally meet.
Cutting our wins, shortening our blessings, speaking our failures, sabotaging our joy, enforcing our own defeat.
Humming "Don't lose heart, don't lose heart...don't let death and pain make you bitter and drive love apart...di worlds already bitter enough, don't let it tek the sweeter piece that is us"
Sometimes all one can do is be there...
Be open to listen, hold, console and care...

Besides Judgment
Has nothing tah do with passion
All the intuition in the world still has a limit of submission and power beyond a certain point...that point being love.
I wonder...
What makes us cold in the midst of the sun.
Our youth brings and reminds us of great expectations, possibilities and
new beginnings—our souls though old in spirit should remain forever young.
The more I feed her need for intellectual seeds of nourishment
I hope her emotional health gains the nutrition it deems.
I desire nothing higher than to inspire and transpire her passion to be her fire's cure.
Heal her heart's wounds and ensure my sincerity never to reopen or create scars anew demure.

June 22, 2012

#65 -- *Just Like That*

Nikki Giovanni says "when I come home if you're not there
I search the air
For your scent…"
Expressions as such So deep,
it leaves me speechless, makes it hard to breathe…
"Lead me on if you must..." as Maxwell bleeds his heart out on the track…
We lose ourselves inside ourselves, searching for that same track…
As the horns bellow and the guitar sings underneath the soulful melody
Our emotions chime along with the trembling keys of the piano in line with each upcoming harmony…
Even in the midst of the darkness, your light shines through the depth illuminating the skies…
Smooth tunes, cool wine and chocolate sweets drown the room's tempo as the jazz sounds dig deep in mesmerizing feats of slow

and fast, high and low and every rhythm in between...
Ohhh, these rhythm and blues songs, these feelings a beautiful, warm, savory thing,
they control our tastes, modes and tones…
Sometimes we focus so hard on healing the battle scars of others we abandon our own bandages…
I fear...
I bleed...
I cry...
Often times over think…
I wonder…wonder so steep that my mind escapes me and my heart burrows and sinks,
Down to feet that's almost too deep for it to beat and breathe again…
Then I recollect my thoughts let go of her past and rediscover feeling again…
To be alone,
there's a refreshing independency that we get caught up in until that familiar Jones creeps up…
unknowingly eating away at our pain and absorbing all of our emotions
until one day we wake up stuck…lost and confused…
because yesterday things were simple, last week hearts were distant
and now they're utterly, undeniably, overwhelmingly…..
INtertwined INsync INvolved ENwrapped ENtrapped and INlove….
Just
Like
That…..

I love you without knowing how, or when, or from where. I love you simply, without problems or pride: I love you in this way because I do not know any other way of loving but this, in which there is no I or you, so intimate that your hand upon my chest is my hand, so intimate that when I fall asleep your eyes close.

~ Pablo Neruda

July 24, 2012

#64 -- *The Day I Said I Love You*

Love...
Can cause anesthetic life
Shots of relational adrenaline awake and disseminate an anguished strife.
Faith our only anxiolytic enables us to reach apogee physics and astrological heights.
We all aspire to achieve childhood dreams and desires of success, greatness and happiness
Yet I aspire to love
and vow to always
create before I annihilate
Bless before I curse
Risk before I hesitate
Choose better despite the worse
Laugh before I cry
Live before I die
I rather make love
Eat pasta read poetry relax be free
Sip wine Croon to jazz and R&B 'til we fall asleep
Because Whose to say...I'll live to love her another day.
So my mind infinitely replays never let the love go away.
Never let the love go away.

June 26, 2012

#63 -- *No Return*

Like a storm overblown
Forceful strong overthrown
Her passion takes my past pain for a turn
So I yearn for desires to burn and churn because in love there's no return.
Final sale cupid's expenses keep me spendin'.
Keep me dealin' poker's cards.
My queen hearts only there's no bluffing in these regards.

Never the lazy lover, old fashioned,
I rather crank my ignition than push start.
Because that slow heating sparks my adrenaline more in that I get a rise as the engine roars
Engaging gauges so these enduring steering words naturally escape my lips because this vibrating kiss
Rides so effortless
one insists
that just maybe this won't be the first
nor the only but the very last hit and miss.

June 27, 2012

#62 -- *The Highs and Loves*

Wale says sometimes love feels like the slowest form of suicide.
So teary fluid in my eyes cries down cathartic lines
as I cite the rhyme.
Yet I beg to disagree because harsh reality in love's the very thing keepin' me alive.
My pedigree nostalgically requires me to fall in love with falling in love so heartache was predestined as my demise.
And still I CHOOSE never to hide
Never to cheat, never to lie
Never in my sorrow to confide
For I rather persist to believe and fight.
For I only exist to fulfill this imminent infinite plight,
To love, be loved and convince the world that despite
Opposing cultures, beliefs, pasts and pain that we all deserve love's natural right.
So I write...
To instill and rekindle society's fire of faith in the one thing we can never escape--
Love.
As bad as the lows sink it's the blessings in the highs that rise and float our hopes, goals and dreams.
A life without the one you can't live without
isn't a life worth living at all.

Love doesn't kill softly just gradually breaks us down to build us back up before we fall...

June 28, 2012

#61 -- *Indulgence*

My indulgence irreversible
Her sweetness irresistible
I imagine the taste delectable
The scent and texture impeccable...
If I could drown in between her seas
from this earth I'd blissfully take leave...
If only to appease
my quenched fiend I'd give my last breath
to savor love's peach seed...
Mouth watering
Tear jerking
Heart pulsing
Mind numbing
Toes curling
Spine tingling
Stomach fluttering…lip biting peaks...
Sugar rushing Sensationalism makes me weak...
I can't help but to insatiably…indulge thee.

June 30, 2012

#60 -- *Wallbreaker*

I see her potential to love so I assure to push down her walls.
Keeping faith I'm strong enough to break through so one day in love she falls.
If patience is virtue
I'll wait for her 'til kingdom come, her heart my pursuit I pray thy will be done.
Sometimes we hide our vulnerability behind nonchalant attitudes in order to protect pride and prevent heartache.

It's natural to not want to get hurt. It's unnatural to avoid falling in love despite the repercussions state...
So high, the clouds are stepping stones to this poetry a sacred dome
Strength isn't measured in control or discipline. It's measured in courage and your will shown.
Hold on to what's most important to you b/c in any moment your life can be turned upside down or inside out so believe in me.
In breaking walls down we build up the courage to trust our pursuit of happiness and ultimate liberal utopian peace.

June 31, 2012

#59 -- *New Beginnings*

It's not a sin to let me in…
It's not a sin to want love again…
It's not a sin to admit the pain
It's not a sin to lose our way
We love we live…we live to love, fall in and out, never forget, seldom forgive…
What is it that we really want…
…that we really need…
If I tell her it's you…
I can only hope that 1 day she can believe...
your natural sweet perfume…
the light softness of your hair…
the warm savory taste of your lips…
the heartiness in your laugh
the innocence in your smile
and your eyes…
…captivating almond dreams they embrace my fantasies….
Of a new life with her,
Leaving behind every "was, once, when, former and were…"
Just infinite refreshed breaths
Enduring reviving
and immense rejuvenated sets
Of utopian bliss

Bold unknown hopelessly enthroned everlasting passions
of cupid shuffled leveled fashions of romanced entrances of
cultured universal whispers of our confessing adore professing...
my love, *mon amour, mio amore, mi amor...*

July 1, 2012

#58 -- *1/2 Way There*

She's my Frankie Beverly
My babe *mi amor ma cheri*
Like a rainy Sunday afternoon
Or a summer family barbeque
Her love gives me peace and
Instills a warmth so deep inside of me the heat builds
a radiance in each heartbeat.
Her touch like 4th of July fireworks
Igniting my spirit
brightening the darkness
Lighting my soul skies
She is the truth, well at least mine
A gospel so real my soul can't deny the sincerity in her voice.
Angel on earth every moment with her is exhaled bliss
I close my eyes and clear my mind
whenever lips approach for a kiss.
Beauty strength and confidence her will
is power beyond definition.
She embodies sensuality...soul and affection.

July 2, 2012

#57 -- *Te Amo*

I don't tell you *te amo* just to make you smile
or drive your emotions wild...
I don't say *te amo* to try to impress your mind
or bypass dying time...
Ily isn't just a cliché confession simply to get

her undressed and when I say I detest those
who abuse and neglect
this 4 letter profession of (L.O.V.E)...I do...
when I express this, it's not because it sounds good...
My "I love you..."
leaves no judgment
contains no insincere substance
but only indulges
and divulges
how important her heart's content is to me...
aside from God, promising careers,
my only other aspirations are to catch her when she falls and
knock her off her feet
As sudden as it may be
I love her undeniably...
and I'm not ashamed
nor afraid to feel impassioned sincerity
because to fight these emotions
would weary me
and to question love's devotion
would bury me
so I remain attentive in hopes that one day love
would marry me...
and that patience and faith
would carry me
When I say *te amo*
it's an unconditional affection
an eternal blessing
and vow to endow,
commit and be there
when needed the most without objection...

July 3, 2012

#56 -- *Longetivity*

My will for longevity supersedes former convictions
and past relational felonies.
Forever is a long time but I'm in it for the long run....
Definite desires to prosper for I aspire infinite bliss....
Permanent affinity and affection is my demise my addiction,
my intimacy...yet I welcome thy submission because she
acquires my relentless attention...my inevitable kiss
Never one for temporary satisfaction for my lasting attraction
requires intellectual attachment...
Sensual connection...
and spiritual elation...
However far I must travel
However deep I must swim
However high I must climb
…there's no opposition that can alter my view,
slow down my stride or off set my future pursuits...
I want nothing and no one else but she...
careless of her past tragedy, warranty...her heart is my receipt...
her trust I pray to always keep...
as I kneel down and pray on one knee.....
I hope for matrimonial subjections of spending lifetimes forever with me...
I yearn to mend that what was broken, that was shattered...
all that matters is her passionate truth....
about the only way that I know how to come is right straight from my heart....
this is the part where I stop and run away but I can't because my legs are paralyzed in quick sand..incapable to depart....and her love has me mesmerized, sinking me deeper and deeper into ecstasy...
and nothing and no one can save me but Christ himself YET
it is he who destined this fatal happening...
all that you've been praying for baby is now becoming factual
so I dig myself deep into her earthly melody in hopes
to enrapture thee...

but this time it feels greater than it was ever meant to be...
my will for longevity....

July 4, 2012

#55 -- *Fireworks*

You
Are
My fireworks.
The light
of
my darkness
The spark
in
my coldness
You illuminate my skies
Color me every hue
Fire me through the night
Blazing crimson ignitions
As hearts arouse and take flight
My
Fireworks
You
Are.
...and bodies explode and spirits make a plight
To soar and collide and shine to new heights.
You
Are
My fireworks.

July 6, 2012

#54 -- *Us*

Us
You and I
is and will always be "us"

Impenetrable ineffable inevitable
"Us"
Stronger than magnetic attraction
Tighter than elastic force
We defy gravity
Over compensate marriage
Us defines bonds beyond that of
Friendship, lover and spouse
Because us runs its own course, beats at its own drum,
travels its own route.
Us is a foundation that can't be broken unless we let go
Us is a security of peace, trust and confidence
that we too well know
Us knows us inside out upside down and around and around.
Those who try to poke holes or play foes fail to cause us woes
Because when you have honesty, communication and sincerity
no flaws no mistakes are too great or small to end you all.
So as we fall I thank God for us
I pray have mercy on us
I have faith that we'll fight to forgive and forget through difficult
days or nights.
And commit to the *us* that we know to be.
Not The Us that the world sees but the Us that's true
to you and me.

July 8, 2012

#53 -- *Imperfectly Perfect*

Words can't describe thy divine affinity that has watered,
planted and grown for you...
As backward as they come We are a true example of imperfect
perfection...a dream never dreamt but that has come true
and yet I wouldn't have us any other way...
They say...if you want change
you must not be afraid to experience things
outside your comfort zone.
Well we are most definitely left field, the other side of the grass,

out of the box and then some.
We beat to our own drum and the music never flowed so sweet.
A unique bond of all trades…
We defy normal, convey destiny, and divulge truth,
overcoming every feat we're in
Unfortunate events I can only pray
That if I should ever see death before I wake
my spirit will be at peace knowing she will be okay.
...Imperfect perfection
My only heart's selection.
Couldn't want for any better
Even in stormy weather
We still shine together
My earthly piece of heaven
My whenever wherever whatever
Imperfect perfection we may stay
Yet I wouldn't have it any other way.

July 9, 2012

#52 -- *Why Did I Walk Away*

Why did I walk away
To live to see another day
For uprising dismay
Or a love's decay
Why did I walk away
Would it have been so bad to stay
Why did she give me a chance
What was the purpose of breaking my stance
Why did I walk away
What awaited me again
A shattered heart
A broken body
A lost mind
Why did I walk away
I should have never left
Faced my fate with death

And yet new life was met
When I walked away
I don't know why
I may never understand
How God can lead the way then just uproot a master plan
Everything happens for a reason
Everyone serves a purpose
I never want it to end
So that's why I walked away
Because I wasn't ready to leave
Because I truly wanted to be
With you
So I fought to walk away
Because there was far too much for me to live for than to stay
And sink and stray
In the darkness and decay
That is fear and dismay
Why did I walk away
Because in seeing the light I envisioned loves face
and I couldn't turn away so I got up
and walked away
and wholeheartedly chose to live to love another day.

July 10, 2012

#51 -- *God's Shower*

There's something about the rain
that moves me in a way I can't explain.
Maybe its persistent motion which dances and sings sincerely on my windowpane...
each time a different meditated melody orchestrated and played.
Sometimes when I experience pain there's no one left to blame
but the person who allowed their heart to be pierced and tamed.
God's mysterious ways are the only saviors of my relentless faith...
I ask him for His guidance and though I may not see it initially
when it comes it's always on time.

The honest to God truth is
I love her for who she already is and not who she wants to be...
Every flaw every weakness every
fear that makes up she...
I embrace each portion each morsel of her imperfect essence
her genuine presence is a pure blessing to me...My God I pray
that she not only gains what she seeks but moreso of what she
needs...
and I hope that her love floats and that in miracles she still
believes...
For from this love
Life lessons we will perceive...
and wisdom we shall receive...
If only this love can set her free,
My heart
My spirit
My mind can rest at peace...

July 12, 2012

#50 -- *Only Love*

Life can be unfair
Life can be cruel
Life can be sweet
Life can make us fools
Death gives us chance
Death gives us peace
Death gives us truth
Death sets us free
Love is power
Love is strong
Love is hard
Love is long
Hate allows fear
Hate allows shame
Hate allows evil
Hate allows pain

The world will try to shake you
and people will try to fake you
Society will try to break you
and
Money will try to change you.
and yet
it's only love
that gets us through...

July 12, 2012

#49 -- *Declaration of Happiness*

I pray that love invests
in an infinite happiness.
It's crazy how the eyes never lie as much we try to hide what stirs and roots deep inside...
Life precious as the newborns it springs.
As fragile as the illness and weakness it brings
yet we live outside our means as if we're not here today
gone tomorrow.
If we settle in our misery the pain becomes self inflicted...
but I rather persist to get uplifted because time here on earth is borrowed.
We grow we learn we change
Some remain stagnant stubborn and selfish in their ways
But that life is not a life at all for complacency is death.
We need be Always moving always seeking always listening bettering one's self.
That is the true meaning of our existence our potential to succeed in fulfilling our purpose and to work toward healing our faults making our pasts mended.
So the eyes seem to never lie but the mind it be a dangerous navigator...
While the heart directs north and the spirit travels south, the mind takes a route over and outside of the path...
in a time zone unheard
If only we would follow our hearts this world would be moti-

vated by love versus the green paper uprooted from our mother earth.
But ultimately that won't be the way of life in which we prosper,
For I declare that I will forever want more for....
My Father
This land
These people
and you
Beautiful you
if it takes a lifetime
I will fight
and proclaim every rhyme
In ALL that is
True
All that is
Good
and ALL that is
soulfully
L...O...V...E.

July 13, 2012

#48 -- *Faithful*

Like the tide to the seas
I'm faithful
Like the breeze to the trees
I'm faithful
Like the sun to the sky
I'm faithful
Like the moon to the night
I'm faithful
Like the light to the day
I'm faithful
Like the shadow to the shade
Like the rain to the earth
I'm faithful
Like innocence to new birth

I'm faithful
Faithful to thee...
Faithful to she…
Faithful to we...
Faithful.

July 14, 2012

#47 -- *Promise Ring*

A promise
Not a commitment
But an unconditional devotion
To always be there
Whenever
Wherever
Whatever
No matter where life takes us or what God has for our future
I want you to know you will infinitely be a part of me.
And in the case that something happens where my time is cut short and I'm physically unable to love or support you I want you to forever have a tangible reminder of how much you truly mean to me.
I hope this symbol expresses that genuine sincerity and that much more.
I love you Fate and that will never change.

July 16, 2012

#46 -- *As Much Joy as Pain*

I've never told anyone this before but I've often felt like God was punishing me for my lifestyle...
Because it seems like every woman I ever love,
no matter how much I fight
and pray and have faith...
just can't find a way to be with me.
This isn't a pity confession or a plea for sympathy.
It's just as honest as I can possibly be.
And it feels like Love just doesn't love me....
But God is love.......right?
sighs
So why doesn't He protect me from this.
It's like a reoccurring tragedy that won't go away.
Maybe I'm meant to be alone
To Share my love. Teach my faith for the moment and then be left for long.
Problem is I never leave. I just wait.
And wait until the seasons change and in my dreams
I no longer see her face.
They say with time comes healing but my scars
don't seem to fade.
Months from now when like this night it passionately rains
her memory will flow through my brain and I'll exhale and one tear down my cheek will sway.
I can't help but think of What happens if she finds another and falls deeply in love.
How am I to feel knowing that was supposed to be me.
Knowing the love I showed her she now gives to someone new.
Then what does that mean
What am I to perceive
Make me think it's something wrong with me and my love.
Like I'm meant to give it but it's not supposed to be received.
Love, unrequited love may be the death of me.
and yet if I am to be punished for doing what I was created to do
despite the odds despite the walls and despite the fear then I must

accept the consequences...
and adhere
and surrender without regret and shame...
Become a prisoner of my passion
and a slave and faithful servant to
the only thing that has caused me
as much joy as pain
....Love....

July 17, 2012

#45 -- *Crucial Part of Me*

It's as if I can hear her heartbeat from a thousand miles…
The rain stops the sun shines and the heavens open
every time she smiles…
When she's sad my whole world quakes
and the universe begins to shake…
I never want to apologize for never
telling her all that I wanted to say…
This woman's work I can never stray…
.only if time allows I can live to love her another day...
One sweet day…of magical kisses
and captured reminisces of chivalry, blossoms
and symbolic ringsI won't ever take love for granted
because I know too well the unpredictability life brings
I never want to hold a grudge…
I never want to deny her love…
I simply want for her mind to be at peace…
And even if I can't be her everything…
I at least want to be the one
who sets her heart free…
love her endlessly
and despite our differences
or distances
be there relentlessly...
because truthfully
no matter where we be

she will always be
a crucial part of me...

July 19, 2012

#44 -- *Whenever wherever whatever*…

Whenever wherever whatever…
Love recognizes these words like an old R&B song that replays over and over in her mind…
I tell her they transcend every piece of me that is drawn in connection to her free of space or time…
She rolls my soul, intertwines my spirit and sends my body in shock…
while I respect her distance, Heaven knows I only desire to be her rock…
Her home away from home…
her 90s Chicago jazz-infused loves jones…
and yet I yield willingly…
wait as patient as faithful saint…because I can't…
Imagine a life without her…
Like Aaliyah's sweet melody

" don't wanna be
I don't wanna go
I don't wanna do….without cha…"

Which is why like Mary J, I don't mind sayin I love you….
Whenever
wherever
whatever
an unconditional phrase conveying
infinite days and eternal ways that one can express
an everlasting promise vowed not to break…
heard it all before…but not with me.
That's what they all say…only they don't mean as I do,
so trust me….
FEAR is a LIAR
A sickness that is only fed by pessimism …

That's what separates the living from the existing.
Being better when everything seems worse.
One step at a time. Digging deep and pressing on
with high spirits
despite the lows that try to break us down.
Rain or shine…summers through the winter seasons
Whenever wherever whatever …this love doesn't expire
or exhaust…
limitless supply, time and effort given at all costs
An engaged player, in it for the long run, my heart sprints,
relinquishing all blood sweat and tears
because I believe that love will always win
It's the simple things that make us "fall,"
but it's the longevity and persistence that make us stay "in"…
Friends or lovers…
Relationships all pretty much flow in the same deepening
waves…
Effort….consideration…support….and communication
Undying faith…understanding….honesty and second chances
Compromise…loyalty…respect…and selflessness
Simple promises to follow and live by for success
Don't question miracles nor take them for granted…
Possibilities are mind-blowing when you stop analyzing their
sensibility and chance it…
Real love…good love…strong love and "I can't help but smile
when I stare too deep in her eyes" type love…
Never let it go…never let it fade…not even for a second,
dam sure not a day…
Because time doesn't wait
… for no one…here today gone tomorrow
So I remain there for love…
Whenever
wherever
whatever.

July 21, 2012

#43 -- *An Expression*

An expression
Of the blessin
It is to love
and be loved
An expression
Of these sweet confessions
Of carpe diem mental drugs
An expression
Of insightful transgressions
I write
Cite
and indulge
In these expressions
In which I in tune from above
Fore seeing future success
Positive lessons
Learned and adapted
I express
Not to impress
But to profess
peace goodwill and infinite love.

July 21, 2012

#42 -- *Light Shines Brightest in the Dark*

Mind
body
and spirit... a million miles a minute...
So twisted up in life and love sometimes we can miss it...
All I know is these silent prayers
are all that ensures we get lifted...
Blind Faith in better days, lighter loads
and a smoother transition...
Nevertheless,

I thank God for THIS position...
For we have to show contentment in our present before
He brings advancement into future missions.
Succumbed to monthly trials, Engulfed in weekly issues and
Overwhelmed with daily questions...
I Promise these 'if it aint one thing it's another' obligations are
just tests, smaller parts of His greater lessons.
We move sooo fast in day to day transactions sometimes we need
cognitive road blocks to slow motion our reactions...
and though some of these speed bumps seem like threats to our
destination's plans we must not crash and drown away to natural
disasters...
For After the storm comes the dawn...
and light shines brightest in the dark, so know that endless blue
skies RISE in the morn...
Neo-soul queen as she stays faithful to thee one can only plea
that her effortless groove so sensual smooth never cease....I
Used to believe that as much as I was in love with love
that love simply didn't love me...
but time knows better than we and thus
this impassioned moment awaits, so I practice patience,
a virtue I seek to set this captive free
because fate is never too late....
Vibes harmonized to peace...mellow to the most infinite degree,
these soulful physics outweigh our logics limits
And come to configure digits of liberal familiar fidgets ***wink***
of glee
Run away and escape to tranquil melody visions with me
of R&B beautiful surprises and *best you ever hads*
unexpected yet timely enraptured *en amor* fads...
and then when the moment is right you shall finally see...
all that you ever wanted
all that you will ever need
was right there all along...
as imperfectly perfect and heaven-sent as a destined,
spiritual gift could be...

July 23, 2012

#41 -- *Abundantly*

Love so fragile
It can bring both the best
And worst out of us
Make us bleed
Sweat and cry
Make us sing
Dance
And fly…
Love
Only created by the one who loves us most
Love
Spiritually divine
Infinite
Ineffable
And yet so
Simple
Thy epitome of epitome
And ALL that is everything and everyone
Our savior
Our protector
Our friend
Love is who we are
And why we strive so hard to be successful
It's all to be loved and to share love
Because money is only temporary
Power is only for the glory of love
We fight
Day in and day out
For love
When are we at our best
When are we most happy
In love
Yes…it hurts the deepest
And feels the hardest to overcome
But ultimately it is thy only thing

That is worth living
And dying for…
God is love
Know the purpose…and live.
Abundantly.

July 24, 2012

#40 -- *No Regrets*

I hope to know everything hidden behind her captivating smile
The pain
The passion
The desire
The anguish...
The joy
The flaws
The anger...all the while.
To care beyond reason
To fight beyond will
That mind-blowing, body-numbing smile is like poetry in motion
lost in time
Worth the compromise
and the frill...
They say that love's for fools
So does that make us the Jokers
They say women can be cruel
and relationships are like a game of poker.
But bluffing is for the minor leagues and I'd rather deal major.
Because holding bk and saving face in love is like downing
Everclear witho the chaser.
So let's strive in 'no regrets' living and loving
Without the pretending. For the secret to succeeding is in our
hearts not our minds
so why not play harder and start winning.

July 25, 2012

#39 -- *That First Love*

Love,

Ever imagine going back in time to when you first fell in love…
almost perfect
Remember how real and unforgettably addictive
and mesmerizing those emotions felt…
Untainted, unscarred….pure, innocent passion
and unrelenting adoration…
Not to mention those abstract, utopian feelings
wholeheartedly reciprocated…
Remember that babe…
like being in love with your best friend
A love so natural, so divine it's as if it's heaven-sent….
I think that's why I believe so much in the potential to love
and be loved again
Because that sensual high, that passionate inebriation for life
and love that we all experience for the first time
is worth chasing…worth finding again….
Every now and then a trip down memory lane
is necessary to embark on a new beginning
Our pasts don't solely define us
but they dam sure explain where we're going
So let's go far and beyond cognitive knowing
Outside of our pain our fear for showing
Our true selves….scared, bruised and lonely
Let's seek a life, a desire and a feeling like
we once knew before the damage took place
A life like we felt when we first discovered love
in all its mercy and grace
Remember that feeling love…
When…
The sun shined a little brighter
And air smelled a little sweeter
A touch warmed your skin just by the contact
A kiss absorbed your lips, melted on impact…
The rain poured a little softer

AND MUSIC
sighs
Music played so effervescent…it was as if every song was written just for you and how you felt at that very moment…
Unexpected, unpredicted…something you never imagined, never prayed for and yet it was exactly everything you ever wanted….
That first love…….undeniably true…
I only pray that you remember and in those memories you find that love amplified refreshed, rebirthed, renewed…

July 26, 2012

#38 -- *Absence of Intimacy*

It's been almost two weeks since I last kissed love's lips.
And I don't meant to count but
I'm at a point where
I find myself missing our intimacy...
Not to be confused with matching passion marks,
massaged foreplay, assisted showers or even Sex...
Because even though the mere assertive contact of your hand
and lips made me wet...
That's not the intimacy in which I mean
or despite our distance can't forget...
Because sex I can live without but
I miss the intimacy of your affection...
The instinctive way you'd intertwine your body
into mine when we'd lay...
Or my firm warmth in which you'd pull in close
against your soft cool essence at bay...
The affection in your words...the gentle tone in your voice
when you whispered my name...
That affection that can't be forced, taught or tamed...
That's the intimacy I miss...
And though in respect of your wish I can only hope
to be a 'special' friend...
That doesn't change the desires I once aspired
to experience over and over again...

The intimacy that transpired emotions to root anew...
An intimacy that was natural and potent
as the ocean is deep and blue.
It wasn't just in the way we kissed,
The moments we touched,
Or even the occasions we simply stopped and stared...
It's the intimacy pursued of a humble love felt growing
between two beautiful spirits if whom only dared...
An intimacy so intrinsic, so rare.
That it inspires me to name a star after her love and care.
An intimacy and affection that I will eternally internally
seek to regain, cultivate and win...
An intimacy planted yet unfulfilled, awaiting the sun
to shine over its roots to give it new life again.

July 27, 2012

#37 -- *Lovher-Friend*

A part of me believes that you sincerely think of me
as simply a fabrication of your imagination
As if your defense mechanism against love
is convincing yourself that "we" had never existed
and that I'll always be only that special friend.
And yet you not only kept but wore my "symbol of promise."
You held on to the one gift that signified commitment
in a non-committed relationship.
That I will never understand except for the simple fact
that you did and do care deeply for me.
And for that we will always be Lover-friends.

July 30, 2012

(Intro):

About three months ago, I met a beautiful intelligent and ambitiously heartbroken young you. I promised you 100 poems to prove my affection my persistence and my loyalty in pursuing you. As a woman of my word I remained true to my consistency... but in hopes to rescue and mend your heart I somehow pushed you away... so now in respect of your recent request this is it. I only hope that my memory doesn't become just another lost love story that you lock away in your heart forever...and that it meant more than your past encounters; that it symbolized the potential of a genuine opportunity and an even greater possibility...

~~~~~~~~~~~~~~~

#1-36 -- *The Very Last Entry*

The unrequited expression on her face
as she drove relentlessly away
Pierced a hole so deepening in my soul
that my heart sank from shame.
As I gathered what was left of my pride lost
in the tracks of the hot pavement in which she sped off…
Silent heavy tears began to flow down my cheeks
as I remotely gazed thru the early morning darkness
of the lighted streets,
asking what just happened?
Fighting not to look back, knowing love's far gone now,
disappeared in the night without a hint of hesitation,
As heavy as my legs felt I managed to walk away...
aimlessly to the passenger side of my friend's car.
I heard her ask me about what happened
but my body was so numb I could barely respond.
My thoughts were so far gone
that all I managed was to stare through the distance
trying to erase the image of love wanting to leave.
Praying I could make it home without flooding these emotions
~~~~~~~~~~~~~~~

that entrapped me...I closed my eyes and pretended to sleep.
30 minutes later I shuffled in my bedroom peeling off every layer
Reaching for my phone I thought maybe I should call and ask
why or how or maybe even who.
But part of me already knew the answers to every question
and yet I still dialed in hope of hearing her voice.
No answer. No answer.
So I tossed and turned replaying the image of her
driving away with my hand still on the door.
and yet maybe I was wrong
Possibly I came on too strong
But my intentions were pure and meant solely for her good.
and still I lay
Lost and speechless.
And as the afternoon sun hits my face and the thunder
rattles the skies my spirit shakes while
reading love's new message that was pre-destined to open up;
then break a part of me that wouldn't give in to past stabs jabs
pushes and takes.
A message to fully let go and forsake...
…every emotion and devotion that was promised
almost three months ago.
Requested to turn away, strictly
put an end to what never was and even though I wanted more
I was content in being that friend.
…An order to flee and to rid my system of an indifference
that's stricken my cognition.
And as I read these words aloud over and over again it hit me
like a cloud of black smoke and filled up my lungs
until I felt like I would choke.
Grabbing my chest, a wave of love sickness approached and my
body grew weak and my head began to spin then lighten
and at that moment it started to sink in.
It was never about her it was never about me.
It is about us and that disastrous longing we imagine and seek
That savior of feelings that we all never expect but only intend.
An hour later I lay in the same spot, the same space
and the same time that love set "us" free.

Overwhelmed in her blunt honesty, ruptured in her rejection,
clarified in her openness to me…
and still as I write I sit here in a midday daze
of what coulda-shoulda would have been knowing better
than to question God's fate.
Que sera sera (what will be will be)
And though the pieces are scattered throughout,
around and about the memories we shared,
I still can't help but love, support and long to always be there...
Unconditional is a promise I set forth and though as requested,
this may be my last love note,
my heart will continue to cite lyrics and poems
and meditated soulful songs,
of what it was and what it is to love someone
even if they fail to love you in return.

Thy End.

October 1, 2012

NightCap[tivation] ***Part I***

As the night leans in
wine'in down the present's promises
The humid air sticks to chocolate skin
Carrying the weight of day...
and as the evening draws to a close
We tempt to dim the lights down real low then
Persist to Disrobe,
relieving dampened clothes.
Yet As we approach the steaming serenade to refresh the spirit,
soothe the mind and cleanse the body...thoughts begin to flow
And emotions start to stroll
And as the hot water trickles down, the pressures of the week
seem to fade and disintegrate into the steam...
Moments which feel like seconds drown into the melodic meditative sounds fulfilling the bedroom, as the air dries our oiled
skin as it gleams.

and while the sun finally sets taking its last bow, the night
submerges our subconscious and deepening breaths follow
as we lay down in our exhale's glow land glee.
The tempo rises as smooth jazz croons
through the walls rocking our souls to sleep.
With a warm body, cool sheets and a side of rum
and ginger ale enwrapped in me, you let go of all that was,
all that is and simply focus on the "will be".
Kissing your forehead, entangling our limbs,
I'll wait for your lids to fall and surrender to the night's wims
and only then can dreams be sweet and I permit to drift off
'til the morning enlightens love again.

October 15, 2012

NightCap(tivation) ***Part II***

They say the only way to rid fear is to look it in its eyes...
(Ijs) if tonight's my last I'll be damn
if pain meets me @ my demise.
See if actions speak louder than words.
I choose you to fulfill and succeed my every verb...
and if good things come to those who wait,
I'll anticipate your love's awake in good faith's allure.
and Trust my patience will be porch-side ready
once you re-open that bolted door.
We seek that better half, that one to grow old with
and take on the world with passion.
Heaven only knows our heart's desire, so instead of saying
what we want why not put it to action.
Don't allow past damage to make a monster
out of the pure soul that you now bound.
Fallin hard can hurt but new love tends to catch,
helping us regain balance on solid ground.
See as women we often know what we want but are too scared
to pursue but love's hit or miss.
We'd rather exist in care-free comfort zones of fire-wall safety
than take another relational risk.

When all we need to do is try thy unusual
and allow someone to break down that wall brick by brick.

Because we all know that casual is "just that"
and youth fades and that one of these days
monogamy becomes the quintessential dream.
I wish to seek the type of uncontrollable passion
that exceeds casual thrashing and precedes eternal stars
in the skies like a matrimonial beam.
Or is it so hard to conceive, so unnatural to believe...
in a honest, loyal, devoting human being that doesn't
betray, deceive, fake or cheat.
I mean damn...whatever happened to diggin soulfully deep...
Re-discovering our femininity, our sensitivity and trusting
in human decency.
Sometimes we're too proud and strong for our own good,
denying help, advice or taking on infinite independent loads...
Then like ticking time-bombs we let tension build up
'til it explodes.

Beautiful contradictions we can be.
One day we want love.
The next just to be free.
Next week we're soul-searching
and next year we've fallen unhappily.
Fear can tear us down, make us second-guess
what we really want.
But my God, is reflection a blessing
and this poetry my cathartic healing
For now every song that reminded me of love
Instead of changing the tune I listen all the way through willin'.
From sensual to sexual with no warning our emotions sway
Instead of taking em off we simply pull em to the side
then dive in like Songz way
Or make love all night til things get right over diced pineapples
Rozay
Because as much as we like to believe or try to deceive our inner
insatiable beings, the best lovers know that the greatest seks
comes with #love.

Adorn like Miguel you just got to know...
Fluid sensuality erects the purest verbal celibacy so...
Forgive me for…
this lyricism is currently my literal high, my diction orgasm and my vernacular buzz all in one.
My poetic nightcap, inebriated spiritually, gone intellectually, as the night deepens, eyes lower and I've faded to "done."

October 21, 2012

Dear Fate,

I never told you this but well before we met it was your bold, confidence conveyed in your social networking that initially attracted me to you. It seemed as though you were always so self-assured in every picture you posted, every word you spoke and your presence was boldly felt. You came off as unapologetic, witty and aggressive but still able to exude an underlying kinder, softer and sweeter side.

Once I met you in person, all those qualities were embodied and refined in physical divinity. Your attraction is surreal and at first encounter took me off guard. It was like a sensual charm that sparked in your eyes making it hard to divert one's attention for too long in fear of losing all sensibility of your presence.

Now that I know you...it's all those simple yet special things that impress me wrapped up in the deeper unseen side of you. The sensitivity and vulnerability seen in your poetry, the free-spirited assertiveness shown in your style and sexuality; and the integrity and intellect expressed in the depth of your conversation...
...all represent your supreme individuality...what makes you different...special...imperfectly perfect...at least for me you radiate that certain *"je ne sais quoi"* that leaves me infinitely intrigued.
But I can only speak for me.

October 25, 2012

Random. Impulsive...but Real.

Dear Fate,

We're only human and I think it's important that we stay connected to that imperfect part of ourselves. That we never lose touch with the pieces of us that make us vulnerable and open. I usually dismiss these thoughts, which is natural, but when spiritually inclined one can't help but express their truth. Like an emotional Tourette syndrome that if not addressed finds a way to eventually seep out. Sometimes when I pray I ask God why I still feel this way and why these emotions don't seem to fade, especially when they're not mutual. I tell Him that it's not fair how those who had hurt you and took you for granted in your past were able to experience the best parts of you and I who love you unconditionally without the lies, deceit or betrayal never even got the chance to have the real you before the pain turned your heart inside out. I wonder who that young beautiful woman used to be.

I imagine she was devoted, loyal, selfless, nurturing and compassionate in her relational quests for love. I feel as though she wore her heart on her sleeves, prayed for her love more than she prayed for herself and guaranteed her undying attention, grace and protection for those who didn't always deserve it. I only wish I could have known her. I wish we could have met before your heartache, when your love was innocent, unbroken and pure again. Wish I could have been your first taste of real love. Your first introduction to commitment; your first risk of investing your heart in a stranger so that you could know the real thing from the start and evade a path of false lovers who promised eternity but instead enforced neglect, abuse and betrayal. But God didn't bestow time machines for a reason and for greater reasons beyond our understanding you had to go through that pain to get where you are today. Yet that doesn't stop my reflective prayers and it doesn't weaken the what-if wishes that float around the back of my mind.

With that being said, this is more for me than it is for you.

This is no inquiry, no plea and no proclamation. It doesn't even require response. It's just as honest and real as I can be with myself and as your friend.

Sincerely,
~ Jai

P.S. Fate,

Even as brief as our history was, despite where we go or who we love, you and I will always be more than just friends. In our time together we built something special and even if it lacked status, entitlement or longevity it was a relationship that I can never deny. One of my favorite lyrics from Detroit lyricist Big Sean is "I rather work on this thing with you than to start something else with someone new." You rushed to mind immediately, the first time I heard the song; and as passionately desperate and somewhat poignant as that expression is, especially in regard to "us" or what "us" used to be, I can't help the memory it brings. Contrarily, all the past songs "we" used to love I can no longer bear to hear for too long but trust I'm getting there…slowly…but surely. Often my thoughts trail toward what could have been; the times we joked about "domesticating," starting a family, sharing new life…I could see myself with you yet the image which was once clear, began to fade along with your feelings and advocacy for new love.

In celebration of a new year to be alive, and healthy and happy for the most part, I've overlooked the actuality of my blessings. And in these past weeks following my new chance at life I did some soul-searching in the days that we've separated...and in that I attempted to prove to myself that I could be without you, even if only for a day...In the midst of this meditation I realized that though it's a possibility that I can, I genuinely don't desire to.

Even though a part of me believes that you tried to love me, tried not to love me and did in fact love me but just wouldn't conceive it; deep down I know that no matter what happens or where our lives take us, there will never be a day that goes by that you won't be on my mind or in my heart so each night I pray for your ongoing peace and happiness. Is it odd for me to think...to dream... and to hope that possibly on one special day that I would bring a little girl into the world with both our strong spirits, my mellowed passion, and your captivating eyes and infectious smile. Maybe so...and yet still...call me crazy but that eccentric part of me just can't help but wait.

Trust me when I say I am only expressing this as a friend. And I would never ask of you what you're incapable of giving. With that being said, I hope all is well and if you ever want or are in need of anything big or small and it's in my power to give, please never hesitate to ask. As always I'm here, whenever… wherever…for…whatever….

If I never met you, I wouldn't like you.

If I didn't like you, I wouldn't love you.

If I didn't love you, I wouldn't miss you.

But I did, I do, and I will.

~ Anonymous

VII.

"THE REAL THING" (Thy L.O.V.E—GOD)

Soundtracks "Woman's Work" - Maxwell |
"Storm Is Over Now" - Kirk Franklin |
"Love" - Musiq |

Quote *"Love is a symbol of eternity.*
It wipes out all sense of time,
destroying all memory of a beginning
and all fear of an end."

~ Anonymous

Dear God,

I always considered your will for me was to find life's purpose and use my God-given gifts to bless others (the community, youth, underprivileged, etc.) with better opportunities, by helping them find their own purpose and gifts. Yet, now I'm starting to wonder if it's deeper than that. If maybe it's as simple and subtle as to solely love without being loved in return. Teaching and giving without receiving, or learning how it really feels to fall hopelessly in love.

Now don't be confused, I am certainly not one for self-empathy, regret nor pity; but self-reflection, meditation and analysis are a must in order to forgive, redeem and essentially "let go." I once heard a line in a movie where a mother prophesied to her son that "happiness is something you have to look after—and in some sense be a vigilante for"…because if you let it dim, let it fade or simply let it go, even for a moment, it's that much harder to gain back around. All in all, I won't go into minutiae because in all honesty, the following letters, poems, prayers and prose speak for themselves.

A wise person once said that you never give us the people we want, but you give us the people we need; to help us, to hurt us, to leave us, to love us and to make us the people we were meant to be. Ultimately life, love and purpose all encompass some inescapable truths, including patience, wisdom, strength, forgiveness and faith. With that being said, from the bottom of my heart, Lord, I thank you.

May 16, 2009

Great Expectations

Life is full of surprises; the best experiences are trailed
by thy unexpected...
Births deaths marriage falling in love...they're all random yet
purposeful trials of living...
Necessary attributions to who we are and what we become,
How we love and how we behave under the worst of
circumstances.
Faith is a great instrument that precedes great expectations,
...without hope we cease to exist...humans survive
through their beliefs...
Belief that we'll live to see and feel another day...
Belief that life will get better and easier...
Belief that tomorrow is the day to end all bad days,
that's why we keep going,
That's why we work and study and exercise and eat and drink
because we believe that there is a greater purpose…
That there is some sense in this journey called life...
Deep down inside every pessimist has a belief in miracles in
dreams in great expectations...

May 31, 2009

Freestyle "Successful" Cover

They say cryin' takes the pain away
So I'm a make it rain 'til heartache fades away

Cuz' I don't know if I'm a live to see another day
Death racin' up on my heels steady tryin' to break
my natural pace
Never been a quitter, raised to2 be a winner,
all I know is first place
Tryna' impress the next but for them I lack respect
so they opinion didn't matter anyway
Yet dying is not my destiny, it's just a happy ending
for what's 2 come next...
Fighting for my last breath, tryna' leave my final mark,
yet I'm checking out like a game of chess
Dear mama, she, I'd never desert her....
Never hurt her, or think that she was a failure,
which is why I can never fail her...
I paint portraits with these words, modern Michelangelo
If hip hop is a sickness then I am thy original antidote...
Lyrical prophet I break silence, this world is my only mobility
And yes I am the driver, conductor and pilot,
take a ride through the mind of a young prodigy
They say I am an old soul so spiritually I'm around 57
If God takes care of fools and babies then
how am I to secure a spot in heaven
If sex is overrated then I'm a day late and a dollar short...
sleepin' behind a rock
But little do they know while they were out nourishing their
bodies of lust I was feeding my mind of wild dreams of black
presidents name Barack/
Yes I'm quite irregular like a menstrual gone wrong/
Guess that makes me random and unpredictable,
like my life's on shuffle song
Extra ordinary with a side of eccentric, got an appetite for
destruction but still some ingredients missin'...
My mind needs seasoning and I feel this secondary education
isn't providing me the nutrition I'm needin'/
But still I'm a daydreamer, that's why I never sleep cuz
reality is that much sweeter/
But really, I rather be doing neither, in between awake and sleep,
in a state of subconscious paranoia but deeper...

If you can't take the heat get out the kitchen, in that case I leave
the world tomorrow cuz the pressures of society's a menace/
The people complain but no one listens, everyday's a fight for
God's children; we sacrifice but what's the difference, this is
Sudan's everyday but we block it because government tells us
it's to explicit
But that is my reality, I don't expect your pity or empathy/
Conducting future generations, leaving genius notes
and inspiring melodies...doing my civic duty, I help
by composing life changing symphonies...
That is my confession be a blessin', give nothin' lesser
than your best...that is your purpose and our destiny...

November 20, 2010

Lost but Not Gone ("Piece" of Mind)

Hopes for dreamers, dreams for kids, faith's for believers…
I used to give two s—
Life is a b— if you let ha…
She'll control your mind, dominate your heart
so you never forget ha
[Love] please don't blow my high/I'm on cloud9
but your aurora's polluting my skies
Your negativity is death to me-surprised I'm still alive.
For love, I'm a sucka', I love em' deep
but then they find another.
We often fight but never let up
You always right cause' I tend to give up
We deserve unconditional affection but prefer lustful injections
Priorities out of whack, doped up on false conceptions.
Juiced up on wet bottoms and 60 second erections….
Some of us need relationship contraception;
'cause our mentality of intimacy is misguided with casual sex.
We tend to have so much hatred inside that no passion, no
purpose of loves left.
Sometimes I lose all faith in humanity; then realize only one to
blame is the human inside of ME/ self pity is so tragic,

our own worst enemy.
Fear is Lucifer's greatest tool against Gods legacy/
on this road to recovery tryna' live free; seek truth and destiny
Altruistic verses, Baptist bibles and kind smiles
aren't enough to save souls,
WE need a wake-up call, an alarm of worldly corruption
and controversy
Sex, drugs and money, thy American dream/
lust addiction and power—what they gradually bring/
I'd kill for a second chance… but then I'd kill for a third/
perfection is irrational but the strive is novel with word.

Maker says: *"Forget the marijuana I'm all the high*
you'll ever need to soar/
Forget the cars and clothes I'm all the finer things
in life plus more/
Forget the diamonds and gold/I'm all the glamour
you'll ever know/if success is a priceless goal,
then love is that infinite times fold."

Sometimes you got to fall back from the top
and lose yourself to get back at number one.
Sometimes your star player gets off track but then
your second wind kicks in then you're back at number one.
Now I lay me down to sleep I pray the Lord my soul to keep,
I plead for forgiveness and favor and remorse/every night I
repent for my sins and then the next day sin again without force.
Temptation is death and free will is a curse,
what if we were destined to be damned—set up for the worse/
what would be the point then-I'm sayin'…
…love me or hate me I'm still gonna' win; born again,
hustlers skin, self-made champion.
Spirit is relentless, I pray I won't resent this, but I am who I am
and who gives a damn if you contend this….*lost but not gone*….

January 8, 2011

I See You

I see you in the sky, the clouds outline your face
the wind forms your figure.
I close my eyes
Brushed through the air like a painting,
chiseled from the earth like a sculpture,
…indeed you are art.
Thy epitome of sensuous meanings….
Breathless you leave us beings.
Ocean tides rise and crash higher when you're nearby,
Even the trees can't help but turn their branches, as you pass by.
Truly heaven-sent, a miraculous gift from above.
Spread your wings and quench us with your grace and love.
Mellow smooth with the simplicity of the south
and the street edge of uptown.
Refined in all aspects; distinguished beyond recognition
and sound.
Tailored from head to soul, fitted suave an mellow.
Spirit follows me, colors me midnight blue, passion red
and golden yellow.
Tickled by your laugh, your sweet memory lingers
like the smell of homemade Soul food.
Undeniably imperfect yet flawless without a doubt;
still never mediocre or crude.
I see you I see you I see you.
For who you are what you believe why you live
and how you love...
I see you and you are me.
Therefore I am you and I am what I see….

January 16, 2011

GREAT

Life is about choices and we are the masters of our fate
God oversees our destiny, but we are the final voices in how

much we can take
In the end, no one can alter your mood/for happiness
is simply a state....
Of mind, so what do you choose....
Why be good when you can be great win or lose,
fight or surrender, push or fallback
The choice is yours...
Mentally keeping score; three things in life you avoid to succeed.
Thou shall not lie, thou shall not cheat and thou shall not stop
'til you reach your peak
I am my hardest critic and my worst enemy
Therefore I envy me for I am the only thing that prevents me
from fulfilling my true destiny
So whatever it may be, God's always testing me
One step closer to peaking, reaching my full potential
and living my legacy...
Every day's a new adventure, a new learning experience,
a new chance to grow...
Every day I take life's lessons an apply them to the future,
careful not to repeat the same mistakes, but careful to do
whatever it takes to surpass good and master great...

February 20, 2011

While You Sleep

What's in a word, what's in a poem?
What's in a tight verse over the perfect beat
of a classic love song
Day in and day out, night comes, night falls—
always seems so deep, so long
It's the same rotation, never phases,
Sam Cooke blazing—crooning in the background,
Change gone come...
Pressures of life creep into bed with me,
conquering my thoughts,
Penetrating my dreams at my dismay
I exhale the obligations of the next day,

Knowing tomorrow's responsibilities are just a shut-eye away
As I gaze out into the midnight sky I replay the events
of my past life...
My mind reruns the close encounter attractions that caused
my heart to have premature ventricular contractions
Or the bittersweet memories of when those first times began
From first loves to first wins to first losses to first sins
Laying awake as the world turns, rumble and shakes...
I ponder, and then as I fall asleep, I wonder if everyone
feels this way or if God simply designated this insight
for me to intake...sweet dreams.

March 1, 2011

Give Us, Us Free

Give us, us free,
No give us, us dignity
Give us back our Royal African legacy
Once the richest continent in the world, now the poorest
In history!
Once the motherland, the brother land, the no worries
Be happy for every man
Now they made us shame of our homeland made us
Change the traditional ways of our homeland
and made us the blame for the poverty
and sickness in our homeland.
Raped and tortured our women children
spreading a deadly disease which they created
And now young lives are jaded. . .
And now young lives have faded. . .
Our beautiful black culture degraded
Our rich black heritage now tainted. . .
But Black people why haven't we yet made it?
Why haven't we stolen back our pride which was taken . . .?
They were our desperate brother and sister into an early
Grave to gain our diamonds, so we suffer while they sit
Back and get paid. . .

Paid for the rich ancestral riches they took without consent. . .
But I guess with a little green, the rest is just irrelevant
Like generosity, sincerity, and compassion
But then again none of that matters. . .
What's important is that we
Fight our deep depression, and diminish
our secular obsessions of
Frivolous materialistic possessions
and begin making wiser investments. . .
In our children's futures and self –making our own treasures . . .
proving that we are
Incorruptible and unbreakable . . . and rekindle
our native land's once undying
Fire and pride . . .
First we must awake our brothers and sisters
who are lost and dead, subliminal to
The aids epidemic, to poverty to homelessness
and to the orphaned babies who lose there
parents to these tragedies.
So now I interrogate us because we are all we have
we can no longer depend on society to provide our needs. . .
We must lick our wounds, tears and fight our own record battles.
Because this war has been fought since the beginning of time;
before Martin Luther King, Malcolm X,
and the Black Panthers. . . .
Our prejudice and hate dates back to Moses
when the Pharaoh refused to let his people go.
Well now we must let go and close the gap
between African and American.
What does that dash signify between our two identities?
Is that separation a discreet indication that I am just a sincere
addition in a nation of statistical prejudice calculations.
Maybe one way we can make a positive contribution
to the world instead of being a
Statistic of sex, drugs or violence or disease
and evolve into the destined African Kings and
Queens we were born to succeed.

April 30, 2011

Untitled

I'm India's truth, Musiq's half-crazy,
Lauryn's ex-factor, even Sade's sweetest taboo at times
Mostly I'm just the cool breeze across your face
or the light rain tapping on the windowpane
Or maybe the sweet honey you drizzle
in your tea Sunday morning
Externally, quiet and shy but bold and boisterous inside
I paint visuals with words your mind can't perceive…
and then I intricately sculpt passion and desire into weak,
empty and deserted vessels that once occupied hearts
Let's go on a trip where love is infinite,
dreams are realities and life is brand new
Closer to heaven and far away from Miles' saxophone blues....

May 10, 2011

Child of God

F— fame, I just want the fortune listen
Potential will only get you so far without thy ambition
We fight just 2 take care livin' out dreams is the mission
On a spiritual high I pray daily just 2 get lifted
So blessed 2 be humble 'n gifted,
I know mama expects greatness, hoping I don't waste it
Dam I miss liberal pubescence,
worry free easy street adolescence
This world killing our faith a little everyday w/ war,
unemployment & recessions-
And yet I stay faithful 'cause I know the fact
that I'm sheltered fed
And clothed in itself is a merciful blessing.
Ever feel like running….
Just dropping everything and gunning till your legs numb,
your arms get heavy and you lose breath.
S— I don't know what the destination is I just want to go.

Get out and maybe come bk.
they say Pain makes people change well I'm feeling brand new.
Despite it all I hold my head high.
Kick me down, f— me over, break my heart, I'm still gone smile
Still gone shine cause' I'm a child of God.

March 30, 2011

Night Fall

Anticipating night fall
Yearning for love's call
Souls so inclined to weep but instead they sing
Bodies attempt to sleep but the mind fiends
What pushes us away.
What forces us to stay.
Where do broken hearts stray.
Where do shattered dreams fray?
Night fall submits me to pray....
Permits me to have faith in a better day....

July 5, 2011

Simplicity

If curiosity killed the cat then simplicity is where it's at....
Life and love will set us up if we let fear become a trap.
Once upon a time I fell in love with rhyme,
words became a sweet escape,
Then those nouns and verbs freed the hurt
like Maya's caged bird.
And ever since, life's been heaven-sent like poetry in motion.
Love is now devotion and every experience a self-deliverance,
not to mention, a muse.
They say it's the little things that count,
Never really understood what that was all about
'til I had nothing...
Living on dreams, fighting Wu Tang's C.R.E.A.M,

Speeding slow, seeing with eyes closed, striven for living
instead of simply existing.
We get so caught up in the hype that our lifestyles get tight and
The roses go unscented, the night stars unseen
and the little things deemed meaningless.
Now all I desire is to ignite infinite fires of those
who still value the secondary,
The forgotten, the miniscule, simply stated... "The real."
"happily-ever-afters" are dying, schemas of commitment
and matrimony skewed.
Because of society's prying ideal views
of happiness and success.
No longer content with just being our true selves
we lose touch with reality and create fallacies
Of what's really important.
Whatever happened to the classics, natural beauty
and the soulful masses?
I miss everyday people, deep lyrics,
abstract arts and imaginative stories.
No more perplex sets of expressions mio amore,
Just forward transgressions of wholehearted confessions.
…done with sugar coating, overloading
and boring life's potential.
For our time is far too essential to waste.
I want to reach newly innovative heights
like Benjamin Franklin kites, soaring above and beyond
On endless flights unknown like ET phone home.
Keep the complicated, long-winded and
overtly extended lifestyles and excuses.
No longer overwhelmed with the stem complexities
of the calculus of cash, physics of power or chemistry of love.
All I need are the elementary 123s affection, the fundamental
ABCs protection, & the basic birds & the bees' imperfection...
Just give me simplicity... no charades, no gimmicks, no added
tax, it's all free....simply simplicity.

August 23, 2011

Arcadia

Being young and finding love is like traveling
to a new unknown destination every several months or so...
You never quite know where you're going
or how long you're staying but....
...you find a distinct attraction, a special element of that distant
place that separates it from the last and the one before that.
Only you hope that this magical feeling, this un-quenching desire
that grows inside of you in this unimaginable place.
Lives on forever so that you never have to leave
in search of another...
Because at that moment you feel as if no other destination
will ever come close to this experience...
and you hope to God that this time you're right.
...C'est la vie...carpe diem...Que sera sera.

September 6, 2011

Dear God,

As you know, in the summer of 2011, following my college graduation and after months of applying and preparing for my commencement and swearing in of the United States Air Force, I was informed by my recruiter that I had been disqualified because of a voluntary, corrective spine surgery that I had performed in my adolescence.

Since the surgery, which was over a decade ago, I had excelled in several athletics including swimming, basketball, flag-football, cross-country and track/field on middle, high school and collegiate levels. So despite my physical "defect" I am a healthy, 23-year-old young woman of cured scoliosis, with no allergies, mental health disorders, family disease history nor criminal background. I neither smoke nor drink, and I am 5'3, 121 lbs and bench press a max weight of 210 lbs; so no I didn't agree with the medical military branch that my ten-year cured scoliosis was a hindrance for my admission into the Air Force. For all I desired was to make a difference in protecting and representing my country, my south Florida community and the University of Miami.

It wasn't until I received this formal notification of rejection that I perceived the level of strength, drive, persistence and passion that I was capable of in fighting for the opportunity and right to serve my country. From the initial moment I received notice of my disqualification, I began assertively defending my virtuous candidacy and qualifications for the United States military. I pursued the advocacy, recommendation and guidance of my state congress, White House military officials, as well as the president of my university, a former Secretary of Health and Human Services under President Clinton. My hope — to overrule the U.S Military Medical Board's decision.

Seeing the vigor, perseverance and optimism I developed in the midst of this challenging life experience, I gained so much wisdom, ambition and insight on the world, my abilities, and most essentially of myself. I learned that though life can be difficult, complicated and often times unfair, even the things that are out of our control are what ultimately make us stronger and more progressive human beings.

The values and knowledge I learned through this curve ball were priceless and looking back I now understand and accept that it was a challenging though necessary experience that I had to go through in order to enhance my potential and move on to a greater venture and purpose. The significance of this milestone was that I stood up for myself and didn't take 'no' for a final answer. I persevered and used my resources, skills and insight to inquire, defend and protect my rights. Nevertheless, after much time, energy and effort I was still denied acceptance; even after multiple over rulings and the support of a White House Air Force Official Correspondent. Overall, I still left the experience gaining a sense of success because at the end of the day I faithfully and fearlessly strived, persisted and grew to become a better person because of it, and I owe it all to your impenetrable will and grace in my life.

September 9, 2011

Dear God,

My faith often leads me to a place where dreams come true, love is forever money is powerless and death is a celebration of freedom from this dark and twisted world. A place where tragedy is only a myth, hope is necessity and happiness isn't just a state of mind but a constant state of being. Where true love conquers all and everywhere is home and every home is heaven. That's where faith leads me…down a path, an unknown destination directed through indispensable belief. Only you know why or how we live and love the way we do; all in a divine plan, a fore-seen destiny and your indisputable purpose for our life.

Nothing is what it seems and no one is perfect no matter how strongly we want them to be. This is where my faith leads. When I'm numb, lost, distant and scared faith takes me away on a journey far from where I know and I blissfully follow because I'm certain the experience will guide me closer to my destiny; and once that purpose is revealed the world will be in my arms to heal, soothe and to rock to peace.

November 23, 2011

Thankful
(On an Atlanta flight for the Thanksgiving holiday)

This time of year always provokes heartfelt convulsions,
carried by impassioned notions of ineffable emotions.
Yet as winter approaches… and solemn autumn closes…
we find ourselves in familiar,
Stand-still poses where suppressed expressions tend to take over.
While the world takes time to realize subtle blessings,
say grace and recognize loved ones whom they neglected/
So I attempt to avoid the guilty pressures …and instead aspire
to desire love before the new year arrives and settles/
Surprised yet grateful that I have yet to give up
and give in to the struggle that is a relationship/
Beautiful heartbreak—so painfully true…

…your process hurts like hell but your results come out
heavenly new. So gracious to have the opportunity to write this;
to have the chance to miss you and embrace
the wisdom I've gained through past loss.
Ready to move forward without back-tracking,
like I'm missing something.
Finally accepting the blessing that is the present;
the relationships I still possess and the memories which will infi-
nitely be kept. I remember why seasons like this help me
to reminisce, help me to remember first kiss and force me
to want to recreate and relive these unforgettable trips.
Thankful for a second chance at what seems like thy unattain-
able; soaring through miles and miles of feelings
well worth fighting for.
Moments like those are what I'm praying for, missing you
and pursuing bulletproof truth is what I'm gunning for.
Thank you God, for seasons like these, which bring
unspeakable feelings of peace and ease.
I only hope that emotions as deep as these,
one day boomerang back to me/
But if not, at least I was granted the breath
to speak my thanksgiving, peace/

November 26, 2011

Philophobia

Encompassed in junctions of philophobic lovers
who in love can't function.
Swallowed by pride they rather die than lie in vulnerability,
rather deny their lack of humility
Philophobes fear feelings unknown;
Fear that one day their emotions may grow
then forced to reap the heartbreaks they sow.
They say that first love is the sweetest,
but that final cut is the deepest.
If you don't love hard then it's not love at all,
I loathe the lazy lover, they investments be the cheapest.

If love is life then philophobes be the grim reapers.
They shun a good thing because they can't distinguish
the temps from the keepers.
Philophobic lovers' faithful under covers
but when it's time for the unveiling they hide
the legs of others.
Philophobes tend to lose control scared to console fidelity
they'd rather mold their own ideals of monogamy.
Philophobia is nothing more than an excuse
to fight the truth that we all w/hold the desire
to be unconditionally loved.
Insatiably kissed & hugged.
Infectiously dipped & dubbed...
as "taken"...
I always preferred to be stirred not shaken.
Not to be confused and mistaken with lust
because it's not solely the heart-stricken infatuation
that philophobes fear...
It's the mind-numbing, body thumping, heart-pumping
irresistible 8th wonder extra-terrestrial-something
that keeps them from falling in love's just.
We all have loved or tried to love a philophobe.
Some of us played the roles ourselves.
Nevertheless it's wise to know that any "fear"
whether love, failure or loss is surely early emotional death...
never settle for less; nothing to fear but fear itself.

January 18, 2012

Dear God,

About 22 years ago today I was in my mother's womb awaiting my arrival, my journey of discovery and greatness. Even back then I possessed a sacred, unmatched potential that foresaw an unspoken unprecedented destiny and purpose. The world today makes it so easy to be pessimistic, distressed and discouraged. People have lost hope, belief and faith in not only mankind but themselves. Our youth are taking their own lives and drugs, sex and poverty are polluting our communities as well as the world. Your "followers" invest, promote and advocate for hate and discrimination against their "neighbors, their brothers and sisters of Christ and their race"—the HUMAN race—because of their own fears, insecurities and self-hate.

Holy Father, I desire to cause change and make a difference in this world. I need to fulfill this passion to be greater and wiser, stronger and faster than I was yesterday, last month and last year. I yearn for no fears, no procrastination and no negativity to ever be my downfall or setback again. And that if I am to fail it will only be because you needed it to be in order for me to succeed in something better. For I know in my heart that my purpose is greater than what I do, who I love or where I go…it's instilled in what I gain through how I change and make others feel. I need that influence, I crave that inspiration and I long for that growth like a homeless man longs for recognition; but not for the attention, not for the fortune—not even for the power or respect; but simply for the grace, joy and peace of knowing and being reminded of why you are alive and why you exist; for the contentment of knowing that I touched the world with my insight, my knowledge and my senses so that my impact may be expressed as only a blessing. I seek that potential of greatness before I leave this beautiful earth.

I must deeper explore my gifts, talents and skills because I fear my neglect has haunted my conscious and placed a dry spell on my spirit. I must find a way back to pursuing the passions that make me unique, that allure my heart to beat. I love you Holy Spirit and though MOST days I know I may not deserve it but you love me back and never leave my side. And for that I am and will forever be eternally grateful, eternally yours—Amen.

March 21, 2012

Heaven Only Knows

Not perfect but whoever you are,
you will be in every way imagined to be.
Your touch your smell your sound will heighten my mind spirit;

awaken every emotion buried inside me.
Life will be a dream & dreams will be blissful reality.
Every day, every moment, shared good or bad
will grow us closer to live brand new.
Not sure how when or where but when it happens
the earth will stand still and time will stop simply for you.
The sky will rain ecstasy, the tides will wave in new beginnings
and the sun will shine on past pain.
Nothing & no one will penetrate something so miraculous so
inevitable that it's out of our control, only for God to tame.
Only when least expected will the angels come down & shed a
light upon you guiding your grace into my life.
Only then will I know that you are the one meant for me now,
always and forever…
No ifs, ands or mights.
'Til then I will faithfully travel this road alone in this journey
known as my purpose...'til love finds a home & all distractions
are gone...because this "one" that they speak of?
Love, only Heaven knows.

"The reason is that everything—and everyone—is constantly changing. We age, grow, learn, get sick, get well, gain weight, lose weight; find new interests, and drop old ones. And when two individuals are constantly in flux, their relationship must be fluid to survive. Many people fear that if their love is free to change, it will vanish. The opposite is true. A love that is allowed to adapt to new circumstances is virtually indestructible.

Infatuation relaxes into calm companionship, then flares again as we see new things to love about each other. In times of trouble and illness, obligation may feel stronger than attraction—until one day we realize that hanging in there through troubled times has bonded us more deeply than ever before. Like running water, changing love finds its way past obstacles. Freezing it in place makes it fragile, rigid, and all too likely to shatter."

~ Martha Beck.

July 17, 2012

Dear God,

My mind is swirling, churning, trying to grasp what exactly just happened and why or better yet what will happen next. As the music wraps around my emotions tempting my senses I try to remain focused but I can't help but be poetic. I want to sleep. My body yearns for sleep, my appetite's diminishing. Lord, you know I detest fear and weakness something serious. I just want to wake up from this sickness and be healed. I'm hoping the music shuffles to a melody strong enough to upbeat my mental and physical capacity. My head is doin' the most right now—I just want a remedy.

Nevertheless, I'm thanking YOU for strength for knowledge, for faith, for favor, goodwill and grace—undying, amorous faith. For without you I am and have nothing. This life, these materials, this body, these memories are all just temporary. You are the only thing that's real in a world filled with such fiction and disappointment. I love you and I thank you for bringing me this far. I've made a lot of mistakes—who hasn't—but then again we're meant to be imperfect so I embrace these flaws and continue to learn from them. So, if this is what you want for my life then I will succeed to make you, my family and myself proud. I can do all things through Christ that strengthens me. Amen.

July 22, 2012

After the Storm

Mind
body
& spirit... a million miles a minute...
So twisted up in life and love sometimes we can miss it...
All I know is these silent prayers are all that ensures
we get lifted...
Blind Faith in better days, lighter loads & a smoother transition...
Nevertheless,
I thank God for THIS position...

For we have to show contentment in our present before He
brings advancement into future missions.
Succumbed to monthly trials, Engulfed in weekly issues & Over-
whelmed with daily questions...
I Promise these 'if it ain't one thing it's another' obligations
are just tests, smaller parts of His greater lessons.
We move so fast in day to day transactions
sometimes we need cognitive road blocks
to slow motion our reactions...
& though some of these speed bumps seem like threats
to our destination's plans we must not crash
and drown away to natural disasters...
For After the storm comes the dawn...
and light shines brightest in the dark, so know that
endless blue skies RISE in the morn...
Neo-soul queen as she stays faithful to thee one can only plea
that her effortless groove so sensual smooth never cease....
I used to believe
that as much as I was in love with love that love
simply didn't love me...but
time knows better than we & thus this impassioned moment
awaits, so I practice patience, a virtue I seek
to set this captive being free because fate is never too late....
Vibes harmonized to peace...mellow to the most infinite degree,
these soulful physics outweigh our logics limits
And come to configure digits of liberal familiar fidgets ***wink***
of glee
Run away & escape to tranquil melody visions with me
of R&B beautiful surprises & best you ever hads....
unexpected yet timely enraptured *en amor* fads...
and then when the moment is right you shall finally see...
all that you ever wanted
all that you will ever need
was right there all along...
as imperfectly perfect and heaven-sent as a destined,
spiritual gift could be...

July 24, 2012

I Know Who My Father Is

And no He's not your average dad but that's quite fine…
No He doesn't buy me things or call me up from time to time
But trust He always gives me what I need
He's my Alpha & Omega…My rock, my protector, my teacher, my lead…
He breaks me down just to build me up again
He hears my cries, answers my prayers, amends my sin
Consoles my spirit, refreshes my mind, strengthens my will
Instills a peace so soulful deep inside me that it sends chills
My Father is thy epitome of GREAT
And I know who He is
He is the sun and the moon
He is the light and the stars
He is my universe
and everything in its path…
He is my creator….He is ALL
My Father is your Father
Our Father and Their Father…
A Father of Forgiveness
A Father of Strength
A Father of Redemption
A Father of Joy & Pain….
I know who my Father is
My Father IS Love…
AND THERE IS NO ONE LIKE HIM
Because He saved me from ME
He healed my wounds; He helped me grow
And this I not only believe but this I know…
He was there from my first step
To the first day of school, He never left
To the first poem I ever wrote
To the first time my heart ever broke
Yes I Know Who my Father is…
And though He isn't the average Dad
He will always be

Father of the Year, Father of the Century & Father of a Lifetime to me…
My Father Who Art in Heaven
Hallowed Be thy Name
My Father of Wisdom Father of Love Father of Faith...
Amen, Amen, Amen…

July 24, 2012

I Am The Future…

I am Yesterday's Sorrow
and tomorrow's better days…
I am the past's Mistakes
& the Present's heartbreak
But most importantly I am unforeseen destiny
I am Next year's black knight in shining platinum armor,
here to set this world free
Of its self-induced negativity, its self-inflicted tragedy
& ill-stricken jealously
For No bullet, no stab, no wound or attack
can rupture my plan for a greater society
A land of hope, a nation of peace and
a universe of indescribable wonder…
Is what I set to create and transcend
with the help of my people…
Because it is not just one man who can
change the world on their own…
If given a chance our future could be
a glory beyond imagination…
Where love is blind and money is charity versus motivation
And where our spiritual & ancestral history
isn't a lie told through manipulator's eyes…
I AM THE FUTURE
Because I so choose to be…
For we all have choices, obligations if you may…
to fight for what we desire,
For what we love & most of all for what we BELIEVE…

If not me then who?
Who will take the responsibility for this destruction, this violence, this seasoned hate that we've spawn...
Our children depend on our strength, our wisdom
& our fearlessness in their lives relentlessly...
So that they can have the courage & aspiration
to defend our culture, our spirituality and our legacy....
But its starts HERE & NOW...
Yet we cannot drift away from our purpose...
for our tides are unpredictable and who's to say
our time won't be cut short...washed away.
This is why the future...our future is in our hands today
guided by God's great plan to restore our fate
and save our souls from evil, new & old...
Our reflections tell us what we need to know about
what it is to come and what's to be done...
Thus I bask in a soulful ambience, patiently awaiting
a sign of relief, a notion to strap up & prepare for His order
to fight for a world that doesn't support my chivalry...
So....
I AM THE FUTURE...not because of appointment
or vigilance or divinity;
Because if one doesn't take the risk for our children,
then who will conquer man's made misery....
I AM THE FUTURE.

August 24, 2012

Perfect Storm

Out of this world...drifted away in life's curves...
there is nothing like the Perfect storm...
She said my kind was supernatural, my heart and my mind
ab-norm and of an extraterrestrial form...
As the skies gray and winds sway, thoughts swerve
and emotions take flight to a stratosphere shy of cool
Temperatures drop, intellects nonstop, humidity thicker
than the tension in a drug prevention clinic.

And as the day sinks in and the night emerges alter-ego freaks
creep in, anticipating the carefree of familiar faces, numbing
drinks and detached intimacy that weekends bring in.
Time never waits, steady paces of nostalgic fast,
even when it slows down it still finds ways to fly pass
Before we come down we strive for the best and worst things
and those feelings erupt…when at the bottom we come alive
because desperation equates transformation and we realize we're
saved because the only way left to go is up…
Spare the rod spoil the child, universally and perfectly flawed…
Because of self-inflicted facades often times
we seek the forgiveness of others when the only one
who requires our redemption is God.
Ever experience love in the eyes of the perfect stranger,
damaged souls leak from tainted pasts enrolled by their imperfect
lovers who broke promises, trust and hearts so for their atten-
dance you had to pay their history's toll.
Lifted off of timid moments; shifted from childhood atonement;
gifted for adult aspirations to be love's exponent —
while still withholding the consequences of enthronement
as unrequited's proponent.
Faded too long off of mixed dreams and misinterpreted drinks…
and streams of tunnel-visional teams deemed of what-can-you-
do-for me fiends with unsatisfied needs for monetary things.
With the rain coming down,
our conscious goes up, and as the music peaks these pheromones
of drizzling tones attempt to entice and tempt stagnant bones
to make familiar moves of sojourn love jones.
So what makes us connect, what makes words relate,
what makes music dig deep…
the realness, the honesty, the sincerity in the moment,
in the story, in the lyrics conveyed of what we feel,
dream and think; so what does your truth say about you;
what does your life lead when you're long gone?
Did you love
Did you leave
Did you see
Did you believe

Did you fight
Did you live
Did you flee
Did you forgive
Did you laugh
Did you cry
Did you feel
Did you try
Did you run
Did you hope
Did you cope
Did you apologize
Did you recognize
Did you commit
Did you forget
Did you heal
Did you reveal
Did you explore
Did you soar
Did you care
Did you promise
Did you smile
Did you compromise
Did you pray
Did you stay
And yet as the rain comes to end so do we…
with only one life to live, one heart to give, we ask ourselves the meaning of it all…
then in seeking purpose, finding truth and securing faith, we finally break down fear's wall,
and the perfect storm comes anew.

Oct 17, 2012

Personal Quotes

A relationship is a partnership...a spiritual, emotional and physical balance of give and take...your lover must invest as much energy into you as you put into them. Real love...good love should make life run smoother and not make it more difficult. You're like an untouchable team taking on the world in all its glory and struggle. Someone to fight, conquer and win your battles with. A lover, friend, muse and partner in crime…so when the sky is falling they'll be standing right next to you. **#Love.**

Oct 18, 2012

Personal Quotes

Please think about it...If today was your last day...what would you do...where would you go...when would you pray... who would you see...and most of all, how would you love? **#BeImpulsive; #BeFearless; #BeReady.**

Oct 19, 2012

Personal Quotes

You grow you change and eventually mature but never lose the best parts of who you are. The innocent parts that are deep-rooted and untainted. The pure parts that reveal your soul, beliefs and passions. Don't allow pain, misfortune or fear to take away the REAL you. The you that trusts w/o reason...the you that loves unconditionally...the you that takes risks and gives 2nd chances and the you that forgives thy unforgivable. The long-lost piece of you that made you the strong and unique individual you are today...don't lose You. **#Faithfulnewbeginnings.** ***TGIL****

Oct 23, 2012

Personal Quotes

Above all, I want my little girl to know that it doesn't matter how other people feel about you...because what matters most is how you feel about yourself...**#Love.**

Oct 25, 2012

Personal Quotes

I listen, observe, absorb and then analyze…
…but often you never know I'm even paying attention until I open my mouth or stare into your eyes with that look that says everything you thought I didn't know but hoped that I would find out…the things you're too tainted to say, too hurt to think or too scared to feel…

We need to realize that EVERYTHING we want is right there in front of us…Some of us are so wrapped in our trivial, personal issues that we MISS blessings, wisdom and even fate. Your heart's desires are so close, so OMNIPRESENT that if you reached out you'd practically kiss them on the lips.
Your dreams, your goals, your PASSION is waiting for you to wake up and grasp the truth, the joy and the gifts that are passing you by each and every day. God wants us to step out on FAITH and shut the doors of fear, doubt and complacency. Walking contradictions we can be...25 % of us don't know what we want, the other 25% are full of ourselves and the other 50%, well are too damaged to go get what they seek, what they know they deserve or worse what they love. You can't complain or ask for guidance when every time He sends you something special you turn it away.

Trust you will never be fully READY to accept a good thing… BUT that's the BEAUTY in a challenge, in change and in what seems like the impossible...we're not supposed to be prepared; and for a person whose always so IN CONTROL of their life... the unseen, the unknown and unpredicted terrify you but it shouldn't... it should excite and IGNITE you…because finally you get that opportunity to fulfill those long-lost, awaited DESIRES.

Open those beautiful eyes and look at what God has placed in your hands, in your mind and most of all in your heart. Every lover, friend, enemy, associate, mentor or muse that He's ever sent you served a greater purpose. Forgive but don't forget... Never let go, pull away or dismiss the internal message, the spiritual signs or the in-your-face direction that leads you to your better future. Love…God has already answered your prayers in advance...don't be too stubborn to feel it, too cautious to think it or too blind to see what's been there all along. **#Love.**

November 2, 2012

Personal Quotes

God has something divine in store for you and I...I can just feel it... from the tip of my mind, to the core of my heart, to every bone in my body & to the depth of my soul...just believe a little longer, the best has yet to come...**#Faithfulazever.** ***ThankGodImLive***

November 4, 2012

Personal Quotes

A positive & reflective conversation has reminded me of the importance of staying true to who you are, what you know & how you feel. We can't judge or control another person's actions, perceptions or opinions. & though we may not accept or agree with them we must always Respect & make the effort to understand them. Because in the end what other people think about how you express, carry & present yourself & those you care for is truly none of your concern.

SN: A bond deeper than friendship, matrimony, even falling in love... There is no stronger symbol of commitment than Family. Can't wait to start my own one day.... **#FearlesslyFaithful**.

Sincerely,
~ Jai

P.S. God,

My heart is so full Lord I can't explain. Through your grace and mercy in my life I've learned to never allow society; the media or religious manipulators tell you who you are or who you should be...live your life. I remember, in a world filled with pain and disappointment you offer a love that never fails.

Lovers, be confident that when you are ready God has the right one for you...and that everyone good or bad that He places in your life is for a greater purpose. From every hair on your head to every bone in your body, to every scar and every flaw there is someone willing & waiting to love you as you are and change your life for the better forever. I now know that "renewal" is an inside job. Great peace and growth starts from within...that deep breath, that silent step back, that reserved moment of free thinking is what brings you closer to self-serenity, relaxation and the calm. For whenever wherever or whatever, remember soul-searching requires nothing and no one but you and God. It starts now....**#Fearlesslyfaithful.**

Theologian Reinhold Niebuhr's ***Serenity Prayer***

God grant me the serenity
to accept the things I cannot change;
the courage to change the things I can;
and the wisdom to know the difference.

Living one day at a time;
Enjoying one moment at a time;
Accepting hardships as the pathway to peace;
Taking, as He did, this sinful world
as it is, not as I would have it;
Trusting that He will make all things right

if I surrender to His Will;
That I may be reasonably happy in this life
and supremely happy with Him
Forever in the next.

I love you. Amen...

"Love is patient, love is kind. It does not envy, it does not boast, it is not proud. It is not rude, it is not self-seeking, it is not easily angered, it keeps no record of wrongs. Love does not delight in evil but rejoices with the truth. It always protects, always trusts, always hopes, always perseveres."

~ I Corinthians 13:4-8a

P.S. *TO MY READERS*

As a writer and an artist, I honestly believe that there is no better way to communicate an idea, thought, or experience, or feeling, than through words and the arts. What interests me most about the arts is the personal connection a writer, artist or performer is allowed to cultivate with their audience. No matter the material, an artist must succeed in capturing and conveying the essence of their subject, and thereby inspiring their audience to go out and positively influence someone else.... So use your gifts, talents, and common sense to contribute to society; this novel may be your comfort, your education, or just pure entertainment...but do take advantage, make a contribution and hopefully someday a difference....

Know that poetry is emotive expression, vividly professing emotional, visual concepts and perceptions...poetry elicits our imperfections...conveying our flaws in each verse, each lyrical wound exudes a commanding verbal presence; a portrayal of our history's pains, struggles and blessings; our deepest thoughts and concerns distressingly in tuned, we are society's lyrical vessels... But what's in a word...? You suppose I'm a decent writer, maybe "great" writer even, because I play with big, fancy words; well pardon my vernacular but what is a word, how substantial is a word if it has no profound meaning; what is a thought if it doesn't spark a deeper sense of knowing and thy unknown. I'm a great writer because of how my words make you feel, the emotions and thoughts and uncertainties I provoke from deep within; that's what makes a paramount writer. Intellect is not defined merely by obtained knowledge; quite simply it's how one utilizes and transforms that knowledge--yes, thy interpretation is the genius of it all. The ability to think, equate, analyze and question for yourself is one of the greatest and most valuable abilities one could and should possess.

Sometimes we feel we're growing and maturing but in reality

while some of us do "adult things" we still—internally—never change. Lost and indulged in our old ways, we remain stagnant and complacent in where we are, what we do and who we engage. Yet while our hearts fight to enhance our minds stay motionless. Like quick-sand we cease to progress and instead continue to push the right people away, pull the wrong advice in and practice the worst behavior.... If we're not careful we may even end up self-inflicting our own pain, misery and failure as well as of those we care for most. We are inevitably a reflection of who and how we love, where we go and live and what we allow in and out of our spiritual worlds. LOVE, always desire more, aspire greater and require better for not only you right now but for you forever more.

God created us all in His perfection and purity; still we are not perfect, but we all are unique and talented in one way or another. Some of us just take longer realizing what that skill is. Some skills we're born with whereas some skills we learn and perfect over time; but nevertheless we are all naturally gifted and all serve a purpose before we leave this world. The profound Bishop T.D Jakes once sermonized: "What purpose do you serve? What do people get when they get you and what do people lose when they lose you?" In life, always remember to leave your imprint on the hearts of everyone you engage; make a lasting, irreplaceable impression.

Be yourself. Above all, let who you are, what you are, what you believe, shine through every sentence you write, every visual you create & every piece you finish.

~ John Jakes

ACKNOWLEDGEMENTS

I've always accepted and believed that God places certain people in our lives to teach us lessons, guide us through struggles, or make us better and/or stronger individuals. With that being said, all credit goes faithfully to my Savior and Lord.

My gratitude extends to those who have and who continue to support me in my endeavors— personal and professional; including my mentors Ni Kal S. Price, Sheri McCurdy-Knox, and Sonja Stephens. Your influence, love, and encouragement in the pursuit of my goals have never been taken for granted; and I sincerely thank you. Furthermore, to my parents, grandparents and siblings, who will always be my biggest fans; and to my closest friends who never doubted me — I could never have come this far without your faith in me.

Additionally, I'd like to acknowledge my publisher, Ms. Linda Samuel and N'Gratitude Publishing Company; who made this aspiration a reality. You have guided me toward fulfilling my childhood dream and lifelong passion: to be an established writer/artist; a successful author; and an inspirational speaker.

Lastly, to anyone who has taken the time to pick up, purchase or recommend my work, my art, and my journey…I thank you for your contribution in making this dream come true.

www.ingramcontent.com/pod-product-compliance
Lightning Source LLC
Chambersburg PA
CBHW030339310726
48979CB00001B/99

* 9 7 8 0 9 8 3 3 1 5 0 3 2 *